Under
Troubled
Skies

Under Troubled Skies

A Western Quest Series Novel

Stephen L. Turner

SUNSTONE
PRESS

SANTA FE

Sunstone books may be purchased for educational, business, or sales
promotional use. For information please write: Special Markets Department,
Sunstone Press, P.O. Box 2321, Santa Fe, New Mexico 87504-2321.

Book and Cover design »Vicki Ahl
Body typeface » Book Antiqua
Printed on acid free paper

Library of Congress Cataloging-in-Publication Data

Turner, Stephen L., 1957-
  Under troubled skies / by Stephen L. Turner.
    p. cm. -- (The Western quest series ; 3)
  ISBN 978-0-86534-750-2 (softcover : alk. paper)
  1. Scots-Irish--United States--Fiction. 2. Texas--History--Revolution, 1835-1836--
Fiction. I. Title.
  PS3620.U76596U63 2010
  813'.6--dc22

                                2009052683

Published in

WWW.SUNSTONEPRESS.COM
SUNSTONE PRESS / POST OFFICE BOX 2321 / SANTA FE, NM 87504-2321 /USA
(505) 988-4418 / ORDERS ONLY (800) 243-5644 / FAX (505) 988-1025

Preface

IN *OUT OF THE WILDERNESS*, volume one of the Western Quest Series, the odyssey of the Turners in America began with the story of Thomas Turner's immigration from Ireland to South Carolina and his struggle to establish a foothold in the wilderness and to cling tenaciously to it.

In volume two, *On the Camino Real*, the story resumes with his grandson, Aaron Turner. The young man falls under the spell of the mysterious, beautiful and dangerous Spanish province of Texas. Through great human effort and bravery, he and his companions are able to establish themselves and their families in a settlement on the edge of Austin's Colony on the Camino Real.

The details of Aaron's life and the exact date of his arrival in Texas are unknown. His participation in the Battle of New Orleans and his acquaintance with historically significant characters are drawn from my imagination.

Under Troubled Skies, volume three tells of his struggles to hold on to what he has gained in the increasingly turbulent and dangerous years leading up to the Texas War of Independence. Here, once again, he encounters his former acquaintance, General Antonio Lopez de Santa Anna, now President and dictator of Mexico, on the battlefield of San Jacinto.

It is known when and where Aaron was born, died and buried. It is known that he was an ordained Methodist minister, a rancher, and a cotton farmer. The names of his first and second wives, his children, and stepchildren are also known. There is a fair degree of certainty where his land was located in what later became Leon County, Texas, near the present day community of Normangee on the banks of the Navasota River. Nancy King Turner, his second wife, lived to a great age with her sons from her first marriage and her youngest son, Aaron Lloyd Turner.

The dates of the great flu epidemic, the Fredonian Rebellion, and the attack of the Cherokee against the Wichita are all historically documented. The dates of Teran's survey, the Mexican Civil War, the atrocities at Zacatecas, the Alamo, and Goliad are well documented. The details of the consultations and conventions, the "Runaway Scrape," and the events leading up to the battle of San Jacinto are also matters of record. Aaron's participation is fictional, but told in a manner consistent with the stories of actual participants.

The probate documents of Aaron's will show that he owned a fairly large amount of farm land where he grew cotton and other crops, as well as raised cattle and horses. It also shows that he was a slave owner, as were many cotton farmers of that period. I have taken the liberty of deleting this aspect of his story.

Although considerable effort has been made to accurately portray life on the Texas frontier, the reader is asked to remember that this is a work of historical fiction and not a history book.

Acknowledgements

THANKS ARE DUE TO MY late cousin, Ed S. Turner of Tularosa, New Mexico, who was responsible for the discovery of the genealogical records upon which much of the family aspects of this work is based, and to my cousin, Ella Turner Bullard, of Callahan County, Texas, our family historian. Thanks are also due to my parents, Aaron Lynn and Alene Combs Turner for their patient proofreading and grammar coaching. They, along with my wife, Roberta, and my children, Aaron Lyles Turner and Melissa Turner DeBusk, have constantly encouraged me to pursue this project. Finally, thanks are due to my editor, James Clois Smith, Jr. and Sunstone Press for their continued confidence and support in this series.

Storming the Alamo

1

October 1826, Navasota Crossing,
Austin's Colony, Texas

THE FULL MOON SHONE brightly in the frosty October night. The air was crisp and still, perhaps too still. Not a bird or animal could be heard from the timber along the river. As was our custom during the month of the Comanche moon, we had taken special precautions. Two men were on guard duty, and the most valuable of our livestock were herded inside the stockade each night.

Tonight, Cody and Nicholas Teel were on duty. Their hunting dogs began to bristle and growl in the direction of the river. Cody saw our uninvited guests first. There were ghostly shadows in the moonlight as several mounted Indians crossed the road on our side of the river slipping silently south. He yelled at his brother, "Indians!" as Nick began to ring the large bell hanging near the gate of the fort.

The baritone voice of the bell rolled loudly through the silent night air. Flickering lights began to appear from one cabin after another inside the fort and at the cluster of buildings along the road a hundred yards to the south.

Cody pounded on the cabin door. "Major, we got Injuns along the river!"

The alarm bell had already awakened me as I grabbed my rifle and pistols. I ran out of the cabin door and bounded up the ladder to the lookout post where the Teel brothers stood on their vantage point above the gate.

As they hurriedly explained what they had seen, I was relieved to notice the lights from the cabins along the road. Someone there was ringing the bell in the church tower in answer to our alarm and to warn those few settlers who lived further south down the river. In the distance, we could hear the smaller bell acknowledging the warning from the distant cabins. At least no one would be caught by surprise.

Everyone knew there was some form of immediate danger. None of us knew the extent or exact nature of the threat. But mounted Indians this time of the year, more than likely, meant the Comanche were on the war path, perhaps in company of their equally dangerous cousins, the Kiowa.

How many were concealed in the timber? Would they see the size of the settlement and leave for an easier prey? Were they raiding for horses? Or were they coming to even the score for something another white man had done to them somewhere else?

As we watched and listened, crashing hooves could be heard galloping north through the trees on our side of the river. A band of ten or twelve riderless horses flashed across the road, closely followed by several mounted warriors. There was no time even to try a quick shot at them, as they disappeared in a single bound across the road.

I could feel my heart pounding and my muscles tensing. "Well, boys, looks like they got the Painter's and Lane's spare horses. Stay here while I make sure everyone else is ready for trouble."

Everyone was wide awake with their guns loaded and ready at the rifle ports in each of the five cabins that made up the fort, including my own. Even the women and older children were armed, too. When it came to fighting Comanche, every one old enough to poke a gun through a firing port would be needed.

If the Comanche had come only for a horse stealing raid, they had done a good night's work. If they had come for scalps, they would be back. It would be a long, sleepless night.

As dawn slowly rolled back the darkness, we saw no sign of our enemies. Were they now watching us from hiding? Had they taken the horses and left?

The families living along the road cautiously appeared from the doors of their cabins, shops, and businesses. All of those buildings were deliberately built on the south side of the road facing the fort one hundred yards away. In the event of an attack, we could provide supporting fire from the fort, as they could for us. That one hundred yards could prove a fatal distance to anyone caught in the open if the Comanche appeared.

Thirteen men and women with a handful of children trotted across the Camino Real and up the lane toward the safety of the fort. Our rifles covered them during their vulnerable trip. As soon as they were inside the gate, the large oak bars were put back in place. Now there were over thirty of us within the stockade who could handle a gun. We would be a tough nut to crack.

Within an hour we could hear galloping horses approaching from the south. From my vantage point above the gate, I could see six riders racing full out up the trail along the river. There were two white men and four white women riding hard for the fort. It had to be the Lanes and the Painters.

"Major, look west!" Cody shouted.

A dozen Comanche warriors appeared from the woods about a hundred yards west of the fort and wheeled their horses south along the river trail at a gallop. This briefly exposed them to our rifles. Shots were fired from all along our western wall. Two Indians fell dead. As the braves drove their horses farther south, Cody took careful aim and dropped one more.

Our horseback neighbors recognized their extreme danger and reined their horses off the river trail onto the open prairie south of the road. The Comanche responded immediately by changing directions to place themselves between their prey and the fort.

This again presented their flank to our rifle fire. Three more fell dead from their horses, but the "wolves" were already among the "lambs." Our friends tried desperately to escape, but the Comanche were having none of it. They were now safely beyond the extreme range of our rifles. We could do nothing more to help. Arrows flew accurately and rapidly from the bows of the charging Indians. Within seconds every member of the Lane and Painter families lay dead.

The Comanche knew they were out of range. They quickly gathered the six saddled horses and returned to mutilate their victims. With rapid, deliberate motions, they scalped each one in full sight of us all. They remounted their war ponies, leading the captured horses behind them. They stopped and wheeled around to face the fort while angrily shaking bloody scalps in their raised fists. With no sense of urgency, they turned their backs to us in contempt and trotted south out of sight.

Gloomy, shocked silence fell over the fort. With an unknown force of Comanche loose along the Navasota, we were powerless to launch a retaliatory raid or even retrieve the crumpled bodies. Anyone who left the safety of the fort risked the same fate that had befallen our friends. Any number of men leaving the stockade would weaken the fort and jeopardize the lives of those who would be left behind.

Every one of us had known the Lanes and the Painters. As maddening as it was, we could do nothing but protect ourselves. All through the long day we stood by our posts. As night fell, we heard coyotes singing their hunting song as they smelled the blood and circled closer to the bodies. An occasional shot from the fort kept the coyotes scared away from the meadow for the duration of the long miserable night.

By the next morning, we sensed our enemies had left. They had accomplished the purpose of their raid. They were returning to their lodges with stolen horses and fresh scalps. They had covered themselves in blood and glory.

A dozen heavily armed men rode out from the fort with the gates barred behind them. Half of them took up positions inside the trading post on the main road. There they could not be surprised and the gun ports on the south wall allowed them to cover the rest of their party as they attempted to recover the bodies. I was in charge of the recovery party. When I saw the mangled bodies, I knew we could not let the women and children in the fort see what the Comanche had done. We buried them where they lay, there in the rich prairie soil. None of us in that detail would ever forget the images of that day or talk about what we had seen.

Once again Texas reminded us that she was still untamed. A land that could be so beautiful, so rich and fertile, could, in the blink of an eye, show her savage and cruel side. This was not a place for the weak or faint of heart. Our paradise was far from conquered.

I was known as Major Aaron Turner, because of my small role at the Battle of New Orleans twelve years ago. I was also known as Reverend Turner, as I was one of the only Methodist ministers in Texas. I was alcalde of the Northeast District of Austin's Colony. We had settled in this beautiful place in 1821. In the five years since, we had accomplished much. Obviously, there was much left to do to secure our futures here.

2

Winter 1826, Navasota Crossing, Austin's Colony, Texas

AS 1826 DREW TO A close, it was evident that Texas was growing and changing with each passing month. More American settlers poured down the Camino Real each day. Stephen Austin had expanded his colony. New colonies were being organized, too. Northwest of Austin's Colony was the Leftwich Colony; to the southwest was DeWitt's Colony. Northeast of us, in an area centered around Nacogdoches, brothers Hayden and Benjamin Edwards had just been granted the right to form another new colony.

Not only Anglos had seen the opportunity for new beginnings in Texas. Indian tribes, which had been displaced by other Indians or white settlers in the ever more populated United States, flocked to Texas. A large number of Cherokee Indians had moved into the northeastern part of Texas. They had already established prosperous farms. The related Alabama and Coushatta tribes had settled into the deep pine forests of far east Texas. From the distant Ohio Valley, Delaware and Shawnee had immigrated to the area along the upper

Sabine and Red River. A group of over eight hundred Kickapoo Indians had come all the way from the Great Lakes region to settle between the head waters of the Trinity and Sabine Rivers.

While the Anglo immigration had been welcomed and encouraged, the Indian newcomers had only been tolerated. These "tame" Indians provided a buffer between the Anglos and the dreaded Plains Indians. The Comanche and Kiowa hated the new arrivals because of their attempts to hunt buffalo on the southern plains that had so long been their private hunting grounds. They attacked the newcomers relentlessly and stole every horse they could grab. Our old friends the Caddo, Tonkawa, and Wichita found themselves crowded by the newcomers and pressed up against the Comanche. Times were very difficult for them; they were caught between a rock and a hard place.

Navasota Crossing was positioned to prosper from the influx of settlers both red and white. Our store was doing a booming business, and the carpenter and blacksmith never saw a slow day. A land office for Austin's Colony had opened within the last year, bringing with it a land agent, clerks, and surveying crews. Two attorneys had come also, as had a doctor, a dentist and a barber. We laughed that there was not a town in Texas big enough to support one lawyer, but not one too small to support two.

Our friend, Robert Contois, known as Captain Rob, because of his years guiding steamboats on the Mississippi and Red Rivers, had established a small community where the Camino Real crossed the Brazos. The muddy Brazos was often impossible to ford in a wagon much of the year. He had built a pair of large ferries which had proven very successful.

He had built a stone cabin with a tile roof above the flood plain of the river. He kept his mules and other livestock in a palisade built to join the back of his house. The three Lane brothers had each taken up land grants on the east side of the river. Each of them had built a cabin on the other three corners of the stockade. This formed a small, but very defensible fort.

The Lane brothers had been shaken by the death of their parents in the recent Comanche raid. None of them wanted to take over the tannery at Navasota Crossing, so they sold it with the cabin and buildings to a new settler. He used the hide pits and cabin for work, but wisely built a small cabin in the settlement on the road. Another family moved in to take over the clay and pottery works left vacant by the death of the Painters. They, too, built their cabin within the relative safety of the others near at hand and close to the protection of the fort.

In late January, 1827, I was awakened by the sound of galloping horses approaching the gate. My stepson, Lucius, had the night watch. He recognized the rider as Tanner Lane on a lathered horse, leading three others.

"Howdy, Lucius! Git the Major for me, will ya? I got important papers for him from Colonel Austin."

I had already thrown on some clothes, and helped Tanner unsaddle his horse and turn all four of them into a stall with water and fresh hay. "What's so important for you to be burning up good horseflesh in the middle of the night? It's forty miles to the Brazos. It must be mighty important."

"Major, all I know is a rider come from San Felipe on a relay of horses. He told Captain Rob to git these here papers to you fast, so he sent me."

"How long did it take you to get here?"

"Purt near six hours close as I can tell. I only stopped to change my saddle to a different horse and take a pee. The horses are worn out and I am, too."

Tanner was one of those people everybody liked. I had liked him since I first met him a few years ago. He was tough as rawhide, scared of nothing, and would do anything for any one. His blue eyes were rimmed in red and his wide shoulders were sagging. "Come on, let's get you something in your belly and a place to lay down."

I led him to the cabin where Nancy was waiting for us. She had warmed up some leftovers and poured a big mug of fresh water for our unexpected guest. He ate like a starving wolf and rolled up in a buffalo robe in a corner of the cabin. He was asleep and snoring loudly within minutes. Nancy joined me at the table where I was reading the dispatches. "Aaron, you look worried. What's going on?"

"There are two dispatches here. One is from the Mexican Commandant of Texas, Colonel Ahumada, in San Antonio. The other is from Stephen Austin." I raised my voice to be heard over Tanner's outrageous snoring. "That boy sounds like a bear with a head cold!" Nancy giggled and we both laughed. "As I was saying, you remember those brothers over at Nacogdoches that were trying to start a new colony?"

"Yes. Edwards, wasn't it?"

"Benjamin and Hayden Edwards. I wasn't too impressed with either one of them. Well, they announced that anybody who was already there needs to prove up the claim to their property or pay a fee to the Edwards to keep their own land. Some of those folks around Nacogdoches have been there a long time, but they don't have a title to their land."

"I was just thinking about Pedro and Juanita Campos. I hope they aren't bothered by this."

"Well, it sounds like dang near everybody is being bothered. The Edwards hired a bunch of filibuster thugs from New Orleans to enforce their policies. They arrested the alcalde, his clerks and Captain Sepulveda back in November and have them locked up in the old stone fort."

"My word, Aaron!"

"Wait. It gets worse. In December, they declared themselves the independent Fredonian Republic. They say they are independent of Mexico, and claiming all the land south of the Red River and everything from the Sabine clear to the Colorado belongs to them."

"Why, that includes our land!"

"They have been burning the homes and farms of people who don't agree with them. They even bribed a couple of bands of

Cherokee to help enforce things."

There was silence in the cabin, except for Tanner's snoring. Nancy looked directly into my eyes, "Why are these dispatches addressed to you, Aaron Turner?"

Diverting my gaze to our sleeping guest and away from Nancy's piercing stare, I replied "Nancy, Colonel Ahumada has ordered me as alcalde of this district to secure the ferries on the Brazos, Navasota and Trinity. He wants me to make sure the Fredonians don't try to move this direction until he can march reinforcements up here. They are bringing a whole battalion up from San Antonio, and the militia from San Felipe is already on the way."

"How bad is this? Are we safe?"

"The Edwards brothers have their hands full with plenty of angry settlers around Nacogdoches for now. Nobody joined up with them like they figured. I don't know how many of those filibusters they have hired, but we know how to handle their kind. I think Navasota Crossing is safe for now. I'm worried about the Campos, though."

Pedro and Juanita Campos were an elderly Mexican couple who lived on a small farm outside of Nacogdoches. I had known them since my first exploration into Texas in 1817. They had befriended us and had frequently provided shelter and food for us on our travels along the Camino Real. They were living in the eye of the Fredonian storm.

After breakfast, I got things organized. Because of recent losses to the Comanche, I didn't want to leave Navasota Crossing vulnerable, so I resolved to take only twelve hand-picked men. The families living on the road would move into the fort while we were gone.

I sent Tanner Lane back to the Brazos with instructions for the militia there to keep the ferries ready for the arrival of the advance group from San Felipe and the main body from San Antonio. Under no circumstances were they to let the ferries fall into the Fredonian's hands. If they were not able to defend them, they were to destroy them. It wasn't likely to happen, but if it did, it would leave us cut off from reinforcements.

Nick, Chance, and Cody would go with me, as would my oldest stepson, Lucius. His brother, Marcus, would reluctantly stay behind to take care of Nancy and the little ones. Seven of the other men and older teens would accompany me. Richard Moore, the blacksmith, would be in charge in my absence. I took the trouble to write out a document recognizing him as deputy alcalde until I returned. I sent Joe Morgan, our carpenter, to visit the villages of our Wichita and Tonkawa friends to enlist their assistance in watching for Indian or Fredonian raiders.

Each of us took saddle bags filled with extra supplies for the road, two rifles, a pair of saddle pistols, extra powder, shot and flints. I carried orders from Colonel Ahumada and Stephen Austin with me. The orders authorized me to enforce martial law and assume command of military and civilian matters until I would be relieved of my duties. It was a huge responsibility.

We pushed the horses and two pack mules hard, reaching the Trinity by dusk. The ferry was in good shape and on our side, the west bank, of the river. We made camp there at the same place we had camped several times in the past. The makeshift corral was still usable as was our shelter. All we had to do was secure a heavy tarp across the top of the frame. The ghosts of our past life and death struggle on this same spot with the Karankawa haunted our sleep. I took the first night watch with Cody. He couldn't sleep either.

"Major, just being here makes my head hurt. We all came pretty near being killed that night."

I remembered how we had fought for our lives in a desperate hand-to-hand fight as the Karankawa had breached our meager defenses. Cody had been wounded. We all had been frightened and carried mental scars of that night.

"I have never liked this place since then, either. It's not just you."

My orders were to hold the Trinity River ferry until the San Felipe militia arrived. If, in my discretion, events required us to do so, we were to proceed directly to Nacogdoches.

About noon the next day, a haggard looking group of four Mexican lancers approached from the east leaving a trail of dust behind them. They didn't wait for us to send the ferry, but swam their weary horses across. An exhausted corporal stumbled from his horse and ordered the other three to dismount. "I am looking for Major Turner."

"That's me, corporal. Looks like you have trouble."

Chance began filling plates with beans and tortillas which he passed around to our unexpected guests. Lucius gathered their horses and unsaddled them in the corral after watering them in the Trinity.

"Thanks be to God we have found you. I can only hope it is in time. The Edwards brothers have Captain Sepulveda, the alcalde, and his clerks locked in the stone fort."

"Yes. So I understand. They have been prisoners for a few weeks. What is different now?"

"They have appointed a new alcalde who has charged them with treason. They are to have a trial soon with a jury of Edwards' hired men. There is no doubt they will hang them, sir. We have been hiding at the farm of Pedro Campos. He told us to find you."

It looked like we would be riding on to Nacogdoches before the San Felipe men arrived. I exchanged the Mexican's tired horses for four of ours. Even though our horses had rested only one night they were better quality and in better flesh than the poor beasts these exhausted men were riding. I delegated four of our men to remain behind to secure the ferry until the San Felipe militia appeared. Austin's letter had said they would be under the command of Abner Kuykendall, who would be under my command until Colonel Ahumada arrived with his battalion.

I told the Mexican corporal to catch a short nap because we would be leaving soon. He and his three men wolfed down their food and slept like dead men. I hardly had the heart to wake them, but an hour and a half later we had to saddle up. We had a long way to go.

We swam our horses across the slate gray waters of the Trinity heading east on the Camino Real at a ground eating trot. We stopped twice to water the horses, loosen their cinches, and let them graze for a few minutes before resuming our travels. Just after dark we stopped for supper. Chance had filled a morral with corn tortillas and jerky. We dared not risk a fire for coffee or warmth for fear of being found by roaming Fredonian patrols. We needed to reach Nacogdoches undetected. We unsaddled and watered the horses, turning them loose to graze wearing hobbles. They rolled in the winter dried grass to ease their saddle-weary backs before grazing. After two hours of rest, we re-saddled the reluctant horses. We could follow the road well enough in the dark. We allowed the horses to proceed at a walk. This enabled us to hear other riders and spare the horses a little.

At dawn we stopped to rest again and eat a little breakfast. Since it was light, we risked a small fire with dry wood that would smoke very little. We made a welcome pot of coffee and fried some bacon. The bacon smelled so good to me, I figured the scent must carry twenty miles on the breeze. Chance made enough tortillas to satisfy our empty bellies, with enough left to feed us the rest of the day.

We continued this grueling pace until we were a few miles from Nacogdoches just before dawn the next morning. We had made a two day trip in only a day and a half. I could not remember being so tired. We made camp in a glade hidden from the road by a dense thicket of pines.

Cody and the Mexican corporal followed game trails through the forest to the Campos farm. Lucius volunteered to take the first watch while the rest of us slept. I wondered where he got the strength. But then I remembered what a remarkable woman his mother, my wife, was in so many ways. The apple had not fallen far from the tree, and I was proud of my stepson.

Cody and the corporal returned about noon. Although it had been a couple of hours, it seemed I had slept only a few minutes. Lucius smiled at my foggy state of mind. Cody made his report. "Major, the Fredonians have already had the trial and are planning to hang the alcalde and Captain Sepulveda at noon tomorrow. I don't know what they are going to do to the clerks. Most of the Edwards' men are drunk as lords in Nacogdoches. I think we can get to the Campos place without any trouble."

As we approached the Campos farm, we heard voices shouting in anger. We arrived to find four rough-looking white men mounted on worthless horses shouting threats at Pedro and Juanita. The Campos had barricaded themselves in their cabin. The barrels of muskets protruded through open gun ports.

The white men were a greasy unwashed and unshaven crew led by a large man with stringy red hair and brown teeth. He roared "We'll burn your cabin down with you no good bean eatin' Meskin squatters inside!"

The twelve of us reined up within easy pistol range of the four men with our guns ready. The stench of stale whiskey and unwashed bodies drifted our way. In their drunken preoccupation they had failed to notice our approach.

"Who the hell are you?" the redhead growled.

"The man who is going to kill you, if you don't all drop your guns right now!" I answered with rage rising in my voice.

"Hayden Edwards sent me to burn these squatters out!"

"The guns. Now!"

As they started to toss down their muskets, the redheaded man suddenly pulled a saddle pistol. A musket shot from the cabin knocked him out of the saddle, dead where he landed. His three companions used the confusion to draw their own pistols. They were all dead before they could fire.

"Pedro. Juanita. It is Aaron Turner. It's safe to come out now."

After the briefest greetings to the Campos, we unsaddled the

Fredonian's horses and turned them loose in the pasture behind the cabin. We buried the bodies in shallow graves in the woods at a place to which Pedro directed us. We discovered two more fresh graves.

Pedro shrugged. "You know it is a good thing you gave me these guns. These bad men came to burn the cabin yesterday, but they changed their minds."

We smiled at Pedro's dry assessment of what must have been a dangerous conflict the previous day. Maybe it was a good thing we had given him a few old guns.

We unsaddled and quickly groomed our horses as Pedro put out fresh hay and corn for them. Juanita fed us like kings while Pedro told the rest of the story. Besides his own adventures, he said the captain, the alcalde, and his clerks, were all still being held in the stone fort. They were to be hanged tomorrow. He thought there were ten or twelve men guarding the fort counting the Edwards brothers. There were other small bands of filibusters camped in various locations near Nacogdoches.

I sent Pedro, Chance and one of the Mexican troopers to make a quick circuit of the settlers who were likely to support us against the Fredonians. When they returned we would put our plan into action. The corporal and two of my men were to post themselves in Nacogdoches where they could observe any changes at the fort.

In the meantime, I put the men to cutting down and trimming a large pine tree about a foot in diameter. Once we had it worked down to a solid thirty foot log, we used ropes to tie handles around it about every four feet with the heaviest rope we could find.

By the time we finished, Pedro, Chance and the trooper had returned leading a group of over thirty well armed and angry citizens. We attached the log to our pack mules and set off dragging our home-made battering ram ahead of our combined force of over fifty men the short distance to Nacogdoches.

Seeing our approach into town, the Mexican corporal and my two other men joined us. They had seen no significant movement in or out of the fort.

A door opened on the second floor gallery of the fort. Three armed men showed themselves. "I'm Hayden Edwards, President of the Fredonian Republic. Who are you men? Are you here to join us or cause trouble?"

"I am Major Aaron Turner, Alcalde of Navasota Crossing, and commander of all the militias of the Republic of Mexico in northeast Texas. I have orders from Colonel Ahumada in San Antonio to place Nacogdoches under martial law and assume command here until the Colonel arrives with his battalion. You are to immediately release your prisoners and place yourselves under arrest."

Uttering profanities, Edwards and his men quickly retreated within the fort. There were only two ways out of the fort: the front door and a set of stairs that led down from the second story to the back of the building. I had stationed men to cover the stairs. Several of Edward's men tried to escape down the stairs. They were ordered to throw down their weapons and surrender. Those that did were taken into custody and unceremoniously hogtied on the ground with rawhide thongs. The others retreated back inside the fort.

By our estimates, those defending the fort were outnumbered at least six to one. Muskets appeared through rifle ports. I detailed men to keep the defenders penned down and cover both doors. Twenty of us grabbed the rope handles of our great pine battering ram and headed for the front door. A single shot from the fort was met by a flurry of musket balls.

When we reached the heavy oak door, we coordinated our movements to slam the log into the door with all our might. The door shuddered and splintered with a rending crack, but did not break through. Our second effort left a bushel basket sized gaping hole in the center of the door. We adjusted our aim for the hinged side of the wounded door. With a loud crash, the door collapsed and fell into the fort. The defenders threw down their weapons and surrendered.

The captain, alcalde, and the clerks were promptly released and the Fredonians took their place in their jail cells. The other

Fredonians camped around Nacogdoches disappeared into the forest night, never to be seen again.

The alcalde stopped me. "Major Turner, years ago you told me that if I ever needed your help you would come to my assistance. You have saved me from the hangman's noose. I will forever be in your debt."

The clerks were reunited with their anxious families and the Mexican captain reported to me. "Major, you are in charge here. My men and I are at your disposal. I owe you my life and I will not soon forget it."

Looking him squarely in the eye, I gave him his orders. "Captain Sepulveda, go to your family tonight. Starting tomorrow, I want you and your men to let every person in this district know that the Fredonians are gone and law and order has been restored."

I left a dozen men to guard the fort and returned to a very weary night's rest in the fragrant hay in the Campos' loft.

Two days later, Abner Kuykendall and thirty men of the San Felipe militia arrived to reinforce us. The fight was already over and the last of the filibusters were gone except those in the jail.

I gave Pedro Campos the four horses and their saddles and tack that had belonged to the dead Fredonians. They wouldn't be needing them. Pedro could keep what he wanted and sell the rest. He kept the best of their weapons, too, with plans to sell the rest.

I attended on the alcalde the next morning. He was brisk and genuine in his greeting.

"I would like to take you up on that favor you had mentioned."

"Anything within my power is yours, Major Turner."

"Do you know Pedro Campos and his wife, Juanita, who live near here?"

"Yes. They seem to be simple, honest people."

"Those simple honest people had a big role in saving you from hanging. I would like you to grant them each a labor of land where they are living. That would be 354 acres. Would that be possible?"

"Of course, Major. I will pay all the fees myself and have my clerks enter it in the book of records immediately."

His clerk produced a map that showed their farm. He carefully marked off two labors.

"Major Turner, my friend and I also owe a great debt to the Campos." The clerk added. "If you do not object, we would like to add a third labor and pay the fees ourselves."

I smiled at their generosity. That would be 531 acres. With the livestock and land, the Campos would lack for little. I nodded my agreement. The signed and sealed legal documents were officially entered in the great leather bound book of records, and the originals were given to me.

"I have known all three of you for many years. You seem to be basically honest men. Do any of you own any land here?"

The alcalde replied, "No. We are not able to afford land on what we are paid."

"As you know, we are still under martial law here until Colonel Ahumada relieves me. As commanding officer, I have rather broad powers to punish or reward citizens as I see fit."

They all three looked down at the floor and shifted nervously in their seats. "I intend to grant one labor of land to each of you two clerks and two labors to you, Alcalde. The fees will be paid from the strong box the Edwards brothers left. However, I want you to choose labors that will border the Campos grant, so that you may protect them from future difficulties."

All three sat in silence. The clerks could not hide their smiles as they turned the great map and began to carefully measure and mark off the plots.

"Major, I do not understand."

"When I did business here, you did not cheat me. You only expected the customary mordida. You have a reputation for fairness and honesty. When the Edwards brothers arrived, you did what was right, and nearly lost your life because of it. This is my way to honor you for your conduct and bravery. I ask only that you continue to act honorably as long as you hold your office. I will add my signature to the deeds as acting military commander so that no one will ever question the validity of the titles in the future."

The alcalde and both clerks rode with me to the Campos farm. They were eager to inspect and survey their own new property, but they waited as the alcalde personally presented the deeds to the Campos. Neither of them could read or write, so the clerks patiently read the documents to them. They then escorted the astonished new landowners on a tour of the boundaries of their new holdings.

The arrival of Colonel Ahumada and his battalion was a welcome event. He thanked me for my good service and relieved me of my responsibilities there in Nacogdoches. The colonel had brought money to pay the militia for their services. They each received four reales for every day of duty. My men were as ready to get home as I was. The alcalde was officially restored to office and the captain gratefully accepted the addition of forty soldiers and two lieutenants to his command. The brave corporal was promoted to sergeant, and each of the other three privates was made a corporal.

It was not necessary to drive our horses as hard on our return trip as we had on our urgent trip east. We gathered the four men we had left at the Trinity ferry, making the trip home in three days. The unaccustomed feel of a few silver coins in our pockets made the ride more enjoyable.

3

Spring 1827, Navasota Crossing, Austin's Colony, Texas

WITH THE ARRIVAL OF spring, the stream of immigrants on the Camino Real reached flood stage. Several settlers picked out tracts of land near Navasota Crossing in all directions. I had earlier filed a claim on behalf of Will Smith. He was the sole survivor of Asa Smith's family after a Comanche raid. The claim was only for a labor of land, but it included the cabin and barns built by his father. He was only seven now, but we held it in trust for him. He was still inseparable from Cody Teel who had rescued him from the Comanche.

In March, a pouch arrived for me from Stephen Austin which contained two letters. The first was a letter of commendation from Anastacio Bustamonte, Secretary for the Interior of Mexico. He expressed the gratitude of the government of Mexico for my role in putting down the Fredonian Rebellion and a commission appointing me Lieutenant Colonel for all of the militias east of the Brazos to the Sabine, and north of the confluence of the Navasota River with the Brazos. This was a huge area, but only thinly populated except for Indians and the city of Nacogdoches. This was an honor indeed, but I hoped it would be more symbolic than an actual responsibility.

Austin had included a cover letter expressing his thanks for reassuring the Mexican government of the fidelity and trustworthiness of Anglo-Texan settlers. I showed the letters to Nancy. She smiled and patted my hand. "The cream always rises to the top."

"Yes, and the turds settle to the bottom. Sometimes I'm not sure which way I'm headed. I think I'll keep these letters to myself for a while."

Later that month a small wagon train entirely composed of only one family arrived in grand style. A wealthy planter from Louisiana, William J. Applewhite, his wife, and five daughters, rolled into Navasota landing like European royalty.

They traveled with no less than six heavily built wagons of the finest quality, each pulled by four of the best matched draft mules I had ever seen. Each wagon was driven by a Negro slave. Leading the wagons was a large spring coach pulled by six matching draft mares driven by another slave and a Negro footman. Mr. Applewhite rode in front of the procession on a fine gaited stallion. A Shorthorn bull of excellent breeding, three milk cows, and a Spanish jack were tied behind the various wagons.

The wagons carried fine steel plows and implements, sacks of seed, including cotton seed, fruit tree saplings, crates of chickens, a young boar hog and six young gilts. There were crates of household goods, furniture and glass windows carefully packed for the jolting trip.

The most amazing freight carried by the wagons was the only cotton gin any of us had seen. It was six feet long and consisted of a pair of great rollers covered with tiny spikes protruding all around. The rollers were turned by a set of iron gears rotated by leather belts made to attach to a circular mill like our grain and sorghum mill.

Mr. Applewhite stopped at Navasota Crossing to have the

spokes and rims tightened on his wagons and some of the harness repaired. The slaves set up a large canvas tent for his family in the meadow south of the settlement. There was a smaller cook tent near it and a couple of tent privies some distance away. He planned to ride ahead to scout out the land he wanted along the Brazos to establish his cotton plantation. He stayed only long enough to get his family settled into their small tent city and to be sociable.

He was a man of middling height and above average weight, balding and somewhat loud. His reddish complexion hinted at a taste for ardent spirits more than days spent in the sun, but his face was set with sparkling blue eyes and a ready smile and laugh. It would be hard for anyone not to like him.

His wife was an attractive woman who was friendly to the people in our community. The Applewhite's daughters were uncommonly pretty. All were tall brunettes with bright eyes and smiles. They ranged in age from seventeen to twenty-two, including a set of twin nineteen year olds. From eldest to youngest were Mary, Emily, twins Katherine and Elizabeth, and the youngest, Miranda.

Mr. Applewhite left for the Brazos riding his fine horse, accompanied by six of his slaves in one of the wagons. He left the coach behind with the two coachmen to tend his family. We also found that the six field slaves had wives and children who had accompanied them in the wagons to our settlement. They made sure that the Applewhite women lacked for nothing.

Cody Teel took immediate notice of Miranda, and the attraction very much appeared to be mutual. Cody had grown into a handsome, tall young man with land of his own, who was well respected by everyone who knew him. His dark hair and bright smile had turned many heads, but Miranda had caught his eye. By the second day they had been camped in the meadow, Cody asked Mrs. Applewhite if he could take Miranda for a buggy ride before supper. Miranda had obviously taken steps to assure a favorable response from her mother.

Cody borrowed a sharp little buggy from one of the two lawyers in town. He was undecided which of the horses or mules to attach to the buggy until his brother, Nicholas, reminded him that a pretty pair of sorrel molly mules needed a little practice in harness. He brushed and curried them until they shone like new pennies. He fitted them in the best harness and hitched them to the buggy.

This just wasn't their day. Both mules were nervous and uncooperative. After some effort and ungentlemanly language, Cody got them under control and pulling together. He took them for a brisk run east on the Camino Real to wear a little of the sass off of them. By the time he arrived for his evening appointment, the mules had their minds on their job. He thought they were pretty well settled down when he pulled up to the Applewhite's large tent.

Cody stepped down from the buggy, firmly setting the brake. After the appropriate pleasantries, he gently handed Miranda up into the buggy and climbed in beside her. She was dressed in pretty clothes proper for a ride in the country and carried a pink parasol.

He clicked the mules into a slow walk. Just as he rounded the corner of their tent, one of the Applewhite's house servants appeared vigorously shaking a soiled rug. The flapping and snapping of the rug set the young mules into frenzied braying, kicking and bucking. Cody expertly sawed on the reins, but the inexperienced team was completely spooked. The race was on. The buggy careened wildly around the meadow. Cody was yelling "Whoa!" to the mules as Miranda lost her parasol. She held on to Cody for dear life, laughing her lungs out.

The mules continued their wild swing as they headed back toward the tents. As the runaway team wheeled and snorted through the camp, the mules side-swiped a canvas privy. The tent ropes hung in the buggy wheels, dragging the remnants of the canvas behind. A shrill scream revealed that Mrs. Applewhite had been on "the seat of ease" when the tent was rudely jerked away.

The mules headed back for their home corral at a dead run. Once through the gate, they brought the buggy to a sudden heavy stop. Miranda was holding tightly to Cody, laughing until she cried. Cody's face glowed red, but her laughter was contagious. He soon was laughing as hard as she was. The sight of Mrs. Applewhite's plight was hilarious, but Cody wondered if he would ever have another opportunity to call on Miranda.

He walked the still giggling girl back to her tent. Mrs. Applewhite was nowhere to be seen. On reaching the tent, Miranda gave Cody a quick kiss on the cheek and disappeared behind the canvas flap. He felt like he was ten feet tall and bullet-proof.

During Mr. Applewhite's absence, Chance wasted no time in courting Amanda. With her mother's permission, they took long walks along the river. He was a frequent guest at their tent for meals. Learning from Cody's disastrous experience, he did not try to take her for any buggy rides. Their visits were encouraged by the excellent food set on their abundant table. Nancy and I smiled at each other to see young love blossoming.

Mr. Applewhite returned after finding the type of land he wanted and filing a claim at the land office. He filed additional claims in the names of his wife and each of the daughters. This provided him with a large tract of choice Brazos River bottom land perfectly suited for cotton production. He planned to grow it and gin it there, then ship the baled cotton down river to sell on the coast.

Blake, Tyler, and Tanner Lane liked his idea of cotton production. They had not broken out much of their grants yet, only enough to grow corn and vegetables, but it also appeared to be prime cotton land. The prospect of unmarried daughters also caught their attention. They contrived some reason to return to Navasota Crossing for a visit.

Mr. Applewhite reported that he liked what he found on the Brazos. It was obvious that the Lane brothers liked what they had found back on the Navasota. Blake and Tyler were soon calling on the twins, while Tanner picked out Emily for his own. Five young bachelors and five eligible young women presented an interesting opportunity.

Mr. Applewhite left to begin building a home for his family on their new land. The Lane brothers returned to start breaking out new fields. The twins and Emily chose to accompany their father to the Brazos. Blake Lane graciously offered his small cabin to them as a home until theirs was completed and he moved in with Tyler. Meanwhile, back on the Navasota, Amanda and Miranda elected to remain behind to keep their mother company.

Six weeks later, Mr. Applewhite returned with his daughters. The Lane brothers decided to ride along with them. He left behind a fully completed beautiful two-story cabin with hewn logs, front and back galleries, smooth-sanded wood floors, and glass windows. He had left his slaves behind to start clearing land for planting.

The first night back, first one, then another, of the five suitors sought an audience with Mr. and Mrs. Applewhite. Each one, with prior planning and consent of their sweethearts, asked for permission to marry. Mrs. Applewhite had been expecting it, but her husband was clueless.

"Why, Mrs. Applewhite, I am shocked at the audacity of these young men to think they could marry our girls, all of them, for Heaven's sake! And the girls are clearly in on this scheme. Why, they have only known each other six weeks."

"Now, William, isn't it wonderful that five, fine handsome young men of character and property are interested in our daughters? We were worried they might become 'old maids' in Texas due to a lack of suitable young gentlemen. If you will recall, we courted only about six weeks before you asked for my hand."

Mr. Applewhite approached me the next morning about performing a combined wedding ceremony in two weeks. I was not surprised and readily agreed. Nancy and I shared a private laugh at the poor man's state of bewilderment.

The girls had ball gowns that would serve as wedding dresses. Plans were advanced for a huge outdoor wedding and dance. Two of our settlers were good fiddlers, and another good with a banjo.

Chance laid out a nice cabin within the fort along the north wall.

With four of us helping him it was soon finished. Cody and young Will scrubbed, swept and brushed their cabin until it was spotless. The Lane brothers did the same with their three small cabins at Rob's little fort on the Brazos.

The day before the blessed event, Mr. Applewhite and the three Lane brothers returned from the Brazos leading three fat steers for the barbeque. The women of the community were busy preparing all manner of food for the festivities. This was a historic event for our settlement.

The weather the day of the wedding was clear, dry and mild. The people of Navasota Landing stood in two large groups with a center aisle left between them. Beginning from oldest to youngest daughter, the brides walked down the aisle hand in hand with their grooms and assembled at the front of the crowd. When I asked who gave these brides in marriage, Mr. Applewhite replied "Their mother and I, and glad of it!"

The ceremony went smoothly and the matrimonial knots were tightly tied. I signed the marriage certificates as alcalde of Navasota Landing. The Mexican government would recognize these as civil unions as long as the couples were all "members in good standing in the Catholic church" which they assured me they were. The word "Catholic" technically means "universal", and as we are all God's children, we could claim to be members of the "universal church." It was a very fine line, but enough so that I was able to sleep at night. For my role as minister at the wedding Mr. Applewhite paid me five silver pesos.

4

Spring 1827, Louisiana Landing, Brazos River,
Austin's Colony, Texas

"H'YA, MULES! GIT UP
Sally! Git up Molly!" The large black man's voice echoed
across the Brazos bottoms. With a hard lunge the oak
stump rolled out of the dark soil. "Dat wad de las one,
sah."

Smiling down from his tall horse, Mr. Applewhite
looked across the newly cleared field. "You boys get
you a drink of water and rest a spell. Then get the mules
hitched up to the breaking plows."

A pair of powerful draft mules was hitched to each
of three breaking plows. The steel plow faces bit deeply
into the virgin native grass exposing the rich dark loam.
The aroma of the freshly turned earth floated up to the
nostrils of the sweating men and mules. They were each
followed by a pair of mules pulling an A-frame spiked
toothed harrow to break down clods and smooth the soil.
Next in the procession was another pair of mules pulling
a two-row lister, laying off the furrows straight as arrows.
Bringing up the rear, a sweating slave drove a pair of
mules pulling a two-row planter, the seed hoppers full
of yellow corn. By the end of the week, they had cleared,

plowed and planted twenty acres of corn.

It was still too early to plant cotton, so Mr. Applewhite sent his slaves, mules and equipment to work the farms of his newly acquired sons-in-laws that joined his own holdings. They planted ten acres of corn on each of their farms.

By May, the process was repeated with cotton. Captain Rob leased his best farm land to Mr. Applewhite, and hired Tanner to tend his livestock and run the ferry. Rob saddled a good horse and led a pack mule. He said he would be gone for a while and didn't know exactly when he would be back.

By July, the "cotton was knee high, and the corn up to an elephant's eye." The six field hands were joined by the two coachmen, four of the female house slaves, and six of the older slave children in the cotton fields along the Brazos. They hoed weeds twelve hours a day six days a week. The heat shimmered across the fields in the hot, humid air. But on this day in July 1827, all work came to a sudden stop. The shrill whistle of a steamboat pierced the sultry calm of the Brazos bottoms. Around the bend of the river appeared a tidy new stern-wheel steamboat, the *Brazos Belle*. The steamer smartly turned her bow toward the east bank and dropped the long loading ramp.

Now the ringing of a bright brass bell joined the noise of the steam whistle. A familiar voice boomed from the pilot house. "Ahoy. Ahoy. Come see the *Belle*!" The voice belonged to our own Captain Rob.

The Lane brothers and their wives gathered at the ferry landing joined by the Applewhites. Rob bounded down the gang plank hand-in-hand with a beautiful brunette. "Isn't she grand? Oh, my wife, I mean. This is Stephanie. And this is my new steam boat the *Brazos Belle*."

"I rode down the river to San Felipe and talked with Stephen Austin. I went down the river a mite farther and met this man, Jared Groce. He has got himself forty thousand acres of prime farm land and a hundred slaves. He is a grouchy ol' cuss."

At that point, Stephanie poked an elbow into Rob's ribs.

"You be nice. That's my father, and he owns half of this precious steamboat."

"Sorry. Anyway, I met Stephanie down at his plantation. He is a big believer in the future of cotton along the Brazos. He convinced me to get a steamboat to haul cotton to Brazosport and the new port out at Galveston. He put up forty-nine percent of the money for the *Belle*. I had to have at least fifty-one percent so the old coot wouldn't boss me around. I'm going to be carrying passengers, freight, and mail up from the coast and cotton, hides, corn, and livestock back down river. Oh, one more thing. In honor of the Applewhites and me being from Louisiana, this community is now officially known as Louisiana Landing."

This met with the approval of all the Applewhite and Lane families. While Rob had been visiting Stephen Austin in San Felipe, he had been appointed alcalde for upper Brazos district. This extended from the east bank of the Brazos at the north boundary of Austin's Colony south to the confluence of the Navasota and the Brazos. He was also made the captain of the district militia attached to my regiment.

Captain Rob set about his duties organizing the militia. There were no other organized settlements in his district, just a few isolated farms, so the militia would come from Louisiana Landing. Mr. Applewhite would serve as the lieutenant. Blake Lane would be the single sergeant, and Tyler and Tanner would be the corporals. At this point, Captain Rob departed from long-held southern tradition. He would train and arm the male slaves. He had to convince Mr. Applewhite first. That would take some doing.

Rob explained the very potent threat of the Comanche. He told him of the death of the Lane brothers' parents. He softened some in his position as long as the guns were locked up except for training and during times of actual threat.

It was done, and the hard hoeing in the fields was interrupted long enough to learn how to load, aim and fire a musket, pistol and shotgun. They practiced until they could hit a gourd hanging in a tree at one hundred yards with a rifle and at thirty feet with a pistol.

Once the men were competent with the weapons, they returned to the hard work in the fields. Then Rob began to train the white women and the female slaves in separate groups. If an enemy came to Louisiana Landing, they would find twenty-nine souls who could handle a gun.

"King Cotton" had come to Texas. Cotton plantations would soon be springing up along the coast, as well as on the Trinity and Brazos Rivers. Along with it came cotton gins, more steamboats, cotton buyers and slaves. Texas would never be the same again. Her people, both white, and of color, would be marked by those changes for generations.

5)

Fall 1827, Navasota Landing, Austin's Colony
Texas

THROUGH THE SUMMER
of 1827, settlers continued to pour down the Camino
Real. Several stayed to settle near us and many others
moved on west. Fall found our corn cribs, hay lofts and
smoke houses overflowing. All of our mule crop sold for
top dollar as did our crossbred horses. Nick and Cody
Teel had fifty head of green broke mustangs to drive east
for sale at Natchitoches.

Cody and Chance wanted to take their wives to see
the Applewhites in late November. Nancy and I wanted to
see Rob and Stephanie, too. We left the younger children
and Will in the care of older children. Cody borrowed
the lawyer's buggy and hitched it to our two best light
draft horses. I drove the team, leading my favorite horse
behind the buggy. Chance and Cody accompanied us on
horseback. Not wanting to camp along the way, we left
before daylight to try to make the forty miles in one hard
day.

We stopped to water and rest the horses. The
women had brought a picnic basket for lunch. While

we were eating on old blankets spread on the ground, we noticed the horses became nervous. They all had their ears pointed toward the woods to the north. They stomped their feet and snorted, their nostrils flaring. Instinctively, we reached for our rifles. The source of their anxiety soon became apparent.

An old white-tailed buck, missing his right antler, trotted from the edge of the woods less than a hundred yards away. His muscular sides were damp with sweat, and his head hung down. Two red wolves slowly emerged from the woods behind him. They crouched low to the ground, their tails straight out behind them. They slowly, quietly padded toward the heaving buck.

Sensing their presence, but too tired to run, he turned to face them. He snorted and pawed at the wolves which stayed just out of reach. One crouched down and sprang at the buck's throat. Seeing the threat, the buck reared up on his back legs and made a lethal thrust at the wolf. His horns caught the wolf in the chest and the buck tossed him fifteen feet to the side.

Seizing the opportunity, a third wolf sprang from cover and sank his teeth deep into the buck's thigh. The buck whirled in a vain effort to reach his attacker. The wolf held on firmly as blood poured from the wound. The uninjured wolf and his injured companion lunged for the buck's throat. The life and death struggle was uneven and quickly ended.

Chance and Cody raised their rifles to shoot the wolves. I waved them down. "Let them go, boys. This part of the country still belongs to them for now."

Nancy spoke up. "Aaron, don't you think we need to be getting along now?"

When I saw how pale the three women were, I realized that they had not shared our fascination with the natural violence we had witnessed. They had not become calloused to bloodshed as we had. "Well, ladies, let's be off so that we can get to Louisiana Landing in time for supper." We resaddled the riding horses and hitched up the buggy, reaching the banks of the Brazos just as the sun set.

Rob, Stephanie, the three Lane brothers and their wives joined us for a wonderful meal at the Applewhite's home. We sat in the den and talked late into the night. Rob and Stephanie returned to their cabin and the rest of us had our own bedrooms upstairs. The Applewhite's cabin stood almost one hundred yards north of the road facing the stockade.

Rob's cabin, and the three Lane cabins that formed the four corners, were joined by palisades to form an effective small fort. The stockade would be able to help defend the Applewhite's cabin, which could also support the fort.

The Applewhite's cabin was designed and built to be defended. The windows were protected by heavy oak shutters with gun ports. The doors were also heavy oak with stout oak bars. There were gun ports covering every approach to the house, and loaded guns in racks along every wall. In the event of an attack, a warning bell was to be rung and all family members and slaves were to immediately report to the house. The stockade had a similar plan of defense.

Captain Rob's four man crew lived aboard the *Brazos Belle*. If an attack came, they were to unmoor from the dock and anchor midstream. They were to use their rifles to support the settlement from the safety of the river and to make sure the steamboat was not taken.

Mr. Applewhite was in full form during our tour of their plantation the next morning. "Look at that cotton. Waist high, it is. And it is loaded with fat bolls. That last frost broke 'em open like popcorn in a hot skillet."

"Oh, the cotton gin. You see those long leather belts? The mules turn the shaft that runs the belts, and the belts turn those big rollers. When the rollers turn, they pull the fiber off the seeds. Over yonder is the bale press. The ginned cotton is packed down into tight heavy bales around five hundred pounds. Once they're baled, we load 'em on the steamer and send 'em to market on the coast."

Chance and Cody were too much in awe of their father-in-law to say much, but they nodded dutifully. I had to ask some questions. "William, in this rich bottom land soil, how much cotton do you think you will make an acre?"

"Ah, Reverend Turner, I'm glad you asked. We are expecting fifteen hundred pounds an acre, not counting the seed. That would be about three bales to the acre."

I was shocked. That would be a small fortune. "Please feel free to call me Aaron. How do you think cotton would do on the lighter soils along the Navasota?"

"Aaron, I think it would do quite well. As you say, the soil is somewhat lighter, but I would expect you to make a bale and a half to two bales. I have a gift for you and my wayward sons-in-law. I am giving you enough cotton seed to each plant five acres."

"Well, thank you very much, William. But we have no gin, and it's too far to haul unginned cotton."

"That's also part of the gift. I am giving the three of you a gin. It's already loaded in a wagon ready to go."

"Sir, this is so generous. Do you have any suggestions on getting the bales to market?"

Rob spoke up. "I have an idea about that, Aaron. You got plenty of good timber there that is valuable on the coast. I think you could build log rafts, load them with cotton bales, and float them down the Navasota River down to where it meets the Brazos, and transfer the cotton on to the *Belle* at Jared Groce's plantation. I'll take you, the cotton and the logs down to the coast. The cotton and logs will bring top dollar there. Then I'll bring you back up the Brazos with money in your pocket."

"Rob, how could anybody so ugly be so smart?"

"I reckon it's just a gift!"

It looked like cotton was coming to the Navasota, too, but I suspected it would be on a smaller scale. The women finished their visiting and we headed home.

6

Early 1828, Navasota Crossing, Austin's Colony, Texas

A FEW OF THE CHILDREN at Navasota Crossing had been sick. The doctor called it the "grippe." Whatever it was, these kids were really sick. They had high fever, horrible coughs and congestion, and they just plain hurt all over their bodies. It hit fast and hung on for several days.

I had been breaking out the five acres I planned to plant to cotton. It sure seemed like my back was hurting. Maybe I just injured it doing something. I felt tired and weak, and I soon had a chill. I made a final pass and quit for the day at noon. Nancy looked worried when she saw me putting the mules up.

"Aaron, your face is flushed and your shirt is soaked with sweat. Your eyes are red and watery. Are you hurting?"

"Honey, I feel like I been wallered by a buffalo. I hurt from the top of my head down to my feet. I can hardly lift my hands up to wash them."

Soon she had me in bed drinking chicken broth and sipping willow bark tea laced with a good shot of whiskey. I was cold and shaking all over. But then I would get so hot I couldn't stand it. My bed clothes and sheets were soaked with sweat.

"Aaron, all the children have it, too. I'm worried."

"Maybe some of the other women can help you."

"No, they have it in their houses, too. This is going to be bad."

Nancy patiently nursed us all back to health. But there was a price to pay for her unselfish care. On the day the last child's fever broke, Nancy fell terribly ill. Her fever raged like a furnace and the chills plunged her into rigors of shaking. She took her broth and tonic, but she was fully in the jaws of this beast of an illness.

She seemed to be improving, but a week into the illness she got much worse. Her cough was deep and rattled the cabin. Her fever soared. The doctor said she had a very severe case of pneumonia. I had lost my first wife, Cynthia, to pneumonia and I was terrified that I would lose my dear Nancy.

I cared for her myself. Lucius and Marcus stepped up to take over the farm work, and Louisa, our stepdaughter, cared for the younger children and the house. But I poured myself into fighting Nancy's pneumonia.

Day by day, her fever lessened, only to return at night. But each night seemed a little better than the night before. Her cough rattled her body and hurt her ribs, but she was slowly coughing the corruption up from her lungs. Each day she ate and drank a little more. She lived on scrambled eggs and biscuits. Three weeks into the pneumonia I felt like she was going to make it.

A month after she fell ill, Nancy felt well enough to take a short walk outside the cabin. Many of our neighbors had similar experiences. There were three new graves in the cemetery south of the road. We would never forget the fever of 1828.

That spring, Nick and Kassie had their first child, a boy named Jake. Nancy and I kept our personal loss to ourselves. The pneumonia had caused the miscarriage of our unborn child. Even our children did not know we had been expecting. We would hope for more children later.

When I had been tending Nancy, Lucius and Marcus had worked on breaking out our cotton ground. One morning as they walked the mules up the river road toward the field they found the partially eaten carcass of a young calf in the fork of a tree at the side of the road. All around the tree were the tracks of a large mountain lion. Both checked the priming of their rifles and rode on to the field. Wanting to finish the field that day, they worked until dusk. They left the breaking plow and harrow and rode the tired mules toward home.

As they neared the carcass of the calf they heard a menacing rumble in the over-hanging limbs of a huge live oak. A massive cougar launched himself at the mounted boys. Their mules bolted, leaving the boys flat on their backs and separated from their guns. As the lion bounded toward the helpless boys, an amazing thing happened.

The mules turned on the lion with a deadly vengeance. One mule seized the predator by the scruff of the neck. With a mighty swing, he snapped the big cat's neck. Not content with the quick death, both mules viciously struck the limp cat with their front hooves until it was an unrecognizable mess of fur and bloody gore.

The boys gathered their guns and their wits. They dragged the shattered remains of the cougar into the woods off the road. There was not a big enough piece of it to keep for a trophy. They then led the blood covered mules back to the stall where they carefully groomed them.

They cleaned themselves up as well as they could before returning to the cabin. They didn't want to upset Nancy too much. When they told the story at supper, they told a watered down version of the whole event. Only later did they tell me the rest of the story. After that experience, we always kept at least one mule or donkey in with the cattle to guard against predators.

Nancy gradually got well enough that I could return to my

farm work. Louisa had proved a huge help around the house and with the children. From that time forward, she accepted more responsibility and proved a tremendous asset to her mother and the whole family. It was several years before Nancy seemed to fully regain her strength.

Navasota Crossing took a growth spurt the spring of 1828. Settlers claimed land up and down both sides of the river and along the Camino Real both east and west of the settlement.

A decent two-story inn was built on the road and was frequently full. Our school grew enough that Nancy recruited Mrs. Morgan to be the second teacher. We also now had a second blacksmith and carpenter, both of whom stayed busy.

The clay and tile works left vacant by the death of the Painters had been successfully reoccupied. Pottery from its kilns was in common use locally and also sold widely. Fired bricks appeared in chimneys and new construction. Tile roofs became more common. They lasted forever and were fire-proof.

The Lane brothers sold their parent's tannery, cabin and land on the river. The new owner was able to buy hides over a wide area. There was no shortage of buyers for the well tanned leather goods. A saddle and harness shop opened up next door to the tannery. The quality of his workmanship was excellent. People came from all over the district to buy his finished products and for repair work. Our community was growing, prospering, and putting roots down deep in to the rich Texas soil.

Cody, Chance and I tried planting five acres of cotton each. It grew well, and the size of the acreage was manageable. Once our other crops had been harvested in the fall, we waited for a killing freeze to open the bolls. Our families and children helped pick the cotton. Our gin hummed to life as the mule-powered belts turned the rollers. It was then pressed into bales weighing four to five hundred pounds each for shipment. The fifteen acres produced a combined thirty-two bales.

We cut some choice pine logs from just east of the settlement and built them into a serviceable raft. We decked the top of it with sawn four by twelve inch planks. The deck was just high enough out of the water to keep the cotton dry unless it turned over. We crafted a crude steering oar and cut gum trees for poles to move the raft.

"Major, you think this is going to work?" Chance asked.

"I was kind of wondering the same thing myself," Cody added.

"Boys, I don't know. Captain Rob seems sure it will. I've never done anything like this before, either. I guess we are going to find out or get wet trying."

We used the mules to drag the bales down to the raft one at a time. The bottom layer of sixteen bales was loaded without any real problems, but the second tier proved much more difficult. We had to man-handle them into place.

We had excess corn to sell, so we stacked sacks of corn on top of the cotton. We covered it all with well secured wagon tarps in case of rain. We tied the whole load with sturdy ropes to prevent shifting.

We made a small canvas shelter for ourselves at the front of the raft, and left room for walking along the sides with poles. There was room at the back to work the steering oar.

Marcus and Lucius talked us into taking them with us on the trip. It seemed only fair as they had spent many hours in the cotton fields. Cody's adopted son, Will, begged to go, but was still a little young for the trip. He had become quite attached to Cody's wife, Miranda, so he didn't protest being left very much.

We pushed off on a mild December morning, taking advantage of a rising river and clear weather. We made good time down the river, occasionally using poles to keep the raft centered and using the rear tiller to steer.

Sometimes we had to pole away from overhanging tree limbs. One afternoon we found ourselves wedged under a large live oak limb. We had brought a two-man whip saw for such an event. Chance and Cody climbed into the tree until they reached the origin of the offending limb. It was two feet in diameter. They cut under the branch first to prevent the saw from binding. As they began the top cut, the sharp teeth of the saw bit deeply into the hard wood until the branch gave way with a mighty crack. Unfortunately, the limb landed squarely across our raft. This required a second cut from Marcus and Lucius to free the stranded craft.

"Papa Aaron, we're pretty hungry. How about an early supper?" Lucius asked.

"I guess you've all earned it. Chance, you got anything to cook?"

"Do ducks swim? Of course, I got something to cook, Major. How does fried ham and cornbread sound?"

"Sounds like I'm ready to eat!" With that, Cody tied the raft to a stump, scrambled ashore and started gathering dry wood.

Chance stirred up a good supper and a pot of coffee. After we ate our fill, Cody retreated into the woods to answer nature's call. Within minutes, we heard a blood curdling scream followed by a pistol shot. Before we could recover our senses, Cody came running from the woods pulling up his britches.

We had all grabbed guns thinking we were under attack. Cody's pants fell around his ankles and he sprawled head-first onto the leaf covered ground. "Snake!" he shouted as he tried to regain his clothes and his dignity.

"I was sittin' down on a log tendin' to business when I heard somethin' movin' in the leaves behind me. It was the biggest ol' water moccasin I ever seen, all coiled up and ready to strike. I jumped just in time for him to miss me. I grabbed my pistol and shot that sucker dead as a hammer."

"Did it scare you, Cody?" Marcus laughed. At that point we all fell out laughing at Cody's predicament.

We pushed the raft back into the middle of the river for the night to discourage unwanted visitors, and floated slowly down stream. By morning, the river was a little wider and deeper, with a stronger current. By early afternoon we reached the confluence of the

Navasota with the Brazos. We could hear and feel the deep rumble as the waters collided. We briefly grounded on a sand bar where the rivers dropped their silt, but the long poles and the nudging of the current soon dislodged the raft.

As the sun started to set, we began to pass a huge cotton plantation on the east bank. We realized this had to be Jared Groce's plantation. As we rounded a bend in the river, we saw the *Brazos Belle* tied to a cypress dock, gently puffing smoke from her stacks.

A familiar voice called down from the pilot house. "Ahoy, the raft! Guide that pile of logs along side and tie on." It was Rob, beaming down from the steamer.

We met Mr. Groce that night at dinner. He seemed hospitable, but I sensed that he was a man who was used to getting his way. We slept in a couple of passenger cabins on the *Belle*. The beds felt good and it was nice to be away from the mosquitoes. The next morning the cotton was transferred to the steamer, and the raft fixed to tow behind.

By noon, Rob swung the bow down river and the paddlewheels began to churn the muddy water. "Looks like you boys didn't do too bad with your crop. I rented my plowed ground out for a third of the crop. He made sixty bales, so I got twenty bales to sell and never touched a hoe or got a blister."

"What have you done with the cotton from Louisiana Landing?"

"Major, I haul a load a week down river from frost until it all gets to the coast. We shipped three hundred bales from the Landing. I'll be hauling Mr. Groce's cotton all spring, over two thousand bales."

"Since he is your father-in-law, how come you call him 'Mr. Groce'?"

"Cause the ol' buzzard doesn't like me very much and he hopes the marriage don't work out. Ain't you the nosey little sucker?"

We tied up that night to avoid snags and sand bars, but resumed our trip by daylight. The strength of the stern wheel working with the current moved us along well. Rob was a fountain of news and tall tales. "Major, you remember our ol' friend General Andrew Jackson? He was elected president of the United States. He's gonna take office next month. President! And we fought right along side of him at New Orleans. I guess that kinda makes us famous!"

"And we are gonna be rich, too. This cotton is bringin' seven and a half cents a pound. That's about thirty-five dollars a bale. What are you going to do with all that money, Major?"

"I'm gonna buy me some peace and quiet. Don't your jaws hurt from all that talking?"

Brazosport was a bustling place that smelled of the sea. Steamers and sailing ships crowded the many docks lining the port. It caused me to remember and miss my days at sea.

We sold the cotton, the excess corn and the logs there. Rob wouldn't take a dime for shipping the goods. He took us across to the new port of Galveston. It was built on the long barrier island that protected Galveston Bay. We picked out some things there for our families and neighbors.

We didn't linger, for we were eager to be off for home. Rob had plenty more cotton to haul.

We spent the night with the Applewhites, and the next morning his slaves loaded our goods in one of his wagons. We also borrowed some horses for the trip home. He sent two of his slaves with us to return the horses and wagon. Pulling a heavily loaded wagon, the forty miles to home would require an overnight trip.

I tried to make polite conversation with his slaves. It was apparent they were uncomfortable speaking to a white man. "You fellas been with Mister Applewhite long?"

"I was borned on his daddy's plantation in Louisiana, sah. So was Tom," replied a middle-aged Negro named Zeke.

"I guess he works you pretty hard."

"I reckon he do. But I ain't complaining."

"No, sah. Me neither, sah." Tom added quickly.

"What keeps you from running off after you leave us?"

Zeke looked at me in amazement. "He got my woman and childrens dere. Doan you think dats 'nough reason to go back, sah?" He exchanged a worried look at Tom.

It struck me that their life was so different from mine that I had difficulty understanding it. They simply were not allowed to carry on a conversation with a white man. It just didn't happen in their world and the rules of society imposed on them. And it would be very dangerous to discuss their master in the presence of anyone. I had stumbled onto dangerous ground. I felt compelled to contain my conversation to the weather and farming.

We made Navasota Crossing in mid-afternoon and made use of the ferry. Our wives and families seemed glad to have us home. I delivered the special order merchandise we had picked up for our neighbors and supplies and gifts for my family. I noticed Tom admiring a simple bolt of cloth. I picked up the fabric and two pouches of tobacco. "These are for you for helping out. Let your woman folk share the cloth."

"Sah, we sho do thank ya, but we cain't take it. Massah Applewhite gonna think we stole it."

"I see the problem. Give me a minute. I'm going to write a note to Mister Applewhite thanking him for the loan of the wagon, livestock and slaves. I'm telling him about the fabric and tobacco as an early Christmas present to you. I don't think he will have a problem with that." They smiled and nodded in agreement and appreciation.

7

Spring 1829, Navasota Crossing, Austin's Colony, Texas

IN 1829, THE FIRST newspaper in Texas, the *Texas Gazette*, was established in San Felipe by its editor and publisher, Godwin Cotton. It served as a good source of news and circulated from San Antonio to Nacogdoches. We always looked forward to its arrival.

The *Gazette* brought good news that spring. The Mexican national legislature had passed new laws that exempted homes and tools of immigrants from seizure for debt by non-Mexican creditors for a period of twelve years after entering Mexico. It was the first homestead protection in the civilized world. When word of this statute reached the United States, it opened the border to a flood of thousands of impoverished and debt-burdened immigrants seeking a better life in Texas.

We only thought we had seen a heavy influx of settlers in the past. Now the river of immigration had reached flood stage. This was good for Navasota Crossing, good for Austin's Colony, and good for Texas. There was safety in numbers. And there was prosperity in numbers, too. The demand for our excess crops and livestock was at an all time high. Some of the immigrants chose to stay around our settlement, some filed claims near Louisiana Landing, and many more moved farther west.

A letter arrived from Stephen Austin. I opened it and read it to Nancy in our kitchen.

> Lieutenant Colonel Aaron Turner
> Alcalde, Northeast District, Austin's Colony
> Commander, Northeast Texas Militia
>
> Colonel Turner,
>   You should expect the arrival of a very important visitor from Mexico City. Manuel de Mier y Teran has been sent to Texas to lead an inspection expedition. He will be investigating the infrastructure including roads, bridges, ferries and river boats. He will also evaluate the military capabilities of the whole province, especially along the frontier, as well as each organized militia. He has been given extraordinary authority and possesses a great deal of influence with President Bustamonte. You will make every effort to cooperate with him and to accommodate his needs to the best of your ability. You will meet him on the Navasota River at your settlement and continue with him as far as Nacogdoches. You have always served this colony and this province well. I am relying on you to make a favorable impression.
>
> Stephen F. Austin, Empresario, Austin's Colony, Tejas y Coahuila, Mexico

"Nancy, you remember I had hoped my new promotion was just a courtesy? Looks like it has turned into a real job with lots of work to be done."

Robert Contois was alcalde of the Upper Brazos District, as well as militia commander. I correctly assumed that he had received a similar letter, as had the alcalde in Nacogdoches. I set off for Louisiana Landing to formulate a plan with Rob.

We would begin by clearing obstructions from the Camino Real. Overhanging limbs were removed. Fallen trees were dragged from the road.

Teams of mules with fresnos leveled the high places and filled in the low spots. Places that were especially boggy were filled with enough gravel to make them passable.

Our road crews soon met his at the midpoint between our two settlements. We joined forces and began work as far as the crossing on the Trinity River. Once there, we made sure the ferry was in good working order. We worked on the road east of the Trinity only as far as the actual approaches to the crossing. We were depending on our counterparts from Nacogdoches to do the rest.

With this unscheduled burden completed, we finally were able to turn our attention to our fields. There was plowing and planting to be done. Cody, Chance and I had increased our cotton acres to ten each. The Moore and the Morgan families planted their first five acres each. Some of the other farmers added a few acres here and there.

"Chance, I want you and Cody and Nick to join the boys and me for a ride out to my cattle pastures. Meet me at my cabin for breakfast, saddled and ready to go after we eat."

"Aaron, ain't you gonna tell us what we are going for? You got my curiosity up."

"Nope. It's a surprise. See you in the morning."

They arrived earlier than I had expected and we had to wait a few minutes while Nancy and Louisa finished cooking breakfast. We had bacon, biscuits and ribbon cane syrup with plenty of good coffee. We rode out of the fort and headed north along the river road a few miles to the pasture land where we kept our livestock, except during the time of the Comanche Moon.

We first reached the corner of the rail fence where we raised our mules. Our Spanish jack ran to the fence and issued an angry challenge to our horses. A flick of my whip sent him sulking back to his band of mares.

"Mercy! I ain't seen your good stock in a long time. I stay too busy with my own. Did you raise these mares, Major?" Nick asked in amazement.

"Sure did, Nick. We've been keeping our better heavy built mares with the jack to try to get some good draft mules. Look at this year's foal crop, the yearlings, and the two year old mules."

Cody let out an admiring whistle. "Those are some of the best young mules I've ever seen. I guess we haven't been paying much attention to what you have been doing up here."

Next, we rode farther to our huge cattle pasture. We had been retaining our best heifers in the herd. Each generation had a higher percentage of improved breeding. We now had forty-five high quality cows with our Shorthorn bull. I had kept the best of the crossbred bulls and castrated the rest. These two year old bulls were three-quarters Shorthorn breeding. Our guests stared in appreciation. These were some of the finest cattle west of the Sabine.

"Major, I never saw better cattle. No wonder you've been keeping them hid out up here." Chance remarked. "I remember thinking you were half crazy shipping that bull out here all the way from Georgia, but look what you've got now. I sure need to buy one of your young bulls."

Our final stop was our horse pasture to the north. Here in spring freshened native grass was our magnificent Thoroughbred stallion and our twenty best upgraded mares and their foals. The men all knew the stallion, but it had been some time since they had seen the crossbred mares. I had kept only the very best colts to grow into young stallions; the others were gelded. These two year old stud colts were of excellent quality and ready to be put to breeding.

Nick said, "I've ridden all over Texas and never seen better horses. Will you sell me a two year old stud colt?"

I turned in the saddle and looked at each of them. "No. They aren't for sale. You have been good friends to me for a long time. I have picked out a two year old stud colt for each of you. Besides that, I also have kept back a good two year old high bred bull for each of you, too. Grab a rope and we'll cut them out and lead them back to the Crossing."

The young stallions were halter broke, so they led easily. Roping and leading the young bulls was another proposition entirely. They had only modest horns compared to the wild native stock, but they were muscular and strong. They bellowed and pulled against the rawhide ropes all the way back down the river road. The stallions and bulls would shape our friends' herds for years to come.

In the shimmering heat of a June afternoon, a Negro on horseback swam across the Navasota, not waiting for the ferry. It was Zeke, Mr. Applewhite's slave, and he was in a hurry.

"Major Turner! I needs to find Major Turner!"

Gray Jamison was loafing near the river. "I know where he is; follow me. What's so important anyway?"

"I got a letter to gib him myself. Massah Applewhite said it's important. Take me to him, young massah." Gray slipped up on his horse and led Zeke north along the river road to our cotton field.

I laid down my hoe and told the others to keep working. "I remember you, Zeke. You need me?" He handed me an oiled leather pouch with an inner canvas envelope. The envelope contained a hurriedly written letter from William Applewhite.

Reverend Turner,

Manuel de Mier y Teran, the Secretary of the Interior of all Mexico, is here. He will be coming your way soon. He seems a man of great importance, although he has been kind to us here. Captain Rob is expected back at Louisiana Landing tomorrow with his steamboat. Teran expects to meet with him since he is the alcalde. He plans to have Rob take him up and down the river, then return. He is inspecting everything, so be prepared.

W. Applewhite

Zeke rested his horse and ate a hot meal on the porch before starting home. I gave him a pouch of tobacco and a single peso for his trouble. He shrugged his shoulders and slid them into his pockets. When Teran came, we would be ready.

I took Nancy with me for a buggy tour of the settlement. The crops looked good and our community had an appearance of settled prosperity. Each farm had a small plot of tobacco, mainly for local use, and a little surplus to sell or trade, plus corn and food plots and a large garden. Nearly everyone tended a small orchard. Several of us were growing cotton for export, and every farm was relatively self-supporting for food crops and meat.

Nancy questioned me. "I thought the Mexican government outlawed growing tobacco."

"Well, they used to, but the law changed just this year. Amazing how fast folks took it up." I grinned slyly at her.

Everything looked in order. We stopped by the combination school and church house. School was not in session and the children were working in the fields. The large ornate cross and paintings of Mary and Jesus in their gilded frames were in place. I spotted two Methodist hymnals on the front row of seats and took those with me.

"I don't know, Nancy. Does this look enough like a Catholic church to you?"

"It isn't me that matters. It is whether Teran buys it. Something is missing. We need to put a small table under the pictures of Mary and Jesus with several small used candles and a rosary. I think that would help. He will know there is no priest here. We can't do anything about that."

"Well, if he asks about weddings, I can tell him I perform civil ceremonies as alcalde. I've got a book with all the names, and another with all the births and deaths."

"You better remind everyone not to call you Reverend."

"I'd almost forgotten about that. That could be a little awkward."

We made the rest of our circuit visiting each of the settlement's families. I reminded them they were voting citizens of the Republic of Mexico and good Catholics. They understood the importance of the advice and the need to make a positive impression on Teran.

We had also agreed that at a pre-determined signal, every able bodied man and boy in the settlement was to report immediately to the fort with their rifles and ammunition. The women and younger children were to secure their houses and display shotguns or rifles from the gun ports. Nick and Cody were to gather the horses and drive them into the corral under the protection of the fort. We practiced twice, and by the second try, everyone seemed to know what to do. We were as ready as we could be.

We had assigned Gray, Tanner and Logan to wait far across the river to watch for the approach of Teran's group and to keep them from getting into any mischief in the settlement. Late on a Monday afternoon, the boys galloped to the river's edge and swam their horses across.

Gray, now in his early teens, rode to find me. "Major, they're coming! They'll be here in less than an hour."

Logan added, "They've got a whole troop of Mexican lancers with them and some mounted soldiers carrying muskets."

Tanner added "There is a man with them riding a fancy black horse. He looks like he is the fella in charge. There are a couple of wagons following the rest of them."

"Alright, you boys pass the word. Everyone knows what to do.

Gray, you ride to the school and ring the bell in the tower."

On hearing the bell, the settlers unhitched their stock and put them away before gathering their weapons. Those hoeing in the fields stacked their hoes at the end of the rows. The flag of Mexico was run up the new flagpole at the fort. In just over half an hour, everyone was at their duty stations.

Teran and his entourage arrived to find the ferry waiting on the west bank. He and his officers, along with the supply wagons, crossed on the ferry. The mounted troops swam their mounts across the river.

Riding to our assembly near the fort, the impressive man on the black horse announced himself. "I am Manuel de Mier y Teran, Secretary of the Interior of the Republic of Mexico. This is Colonel Ahumada, military commander of Tejas. Where is the alcalde?"

I stepped forward and bowed as gracefully as I could, removing my hat. "I am Lieutenant Colonel Aaron Turner, Alcalde of the Northeast District of Austin's Colony and military commander of the militias in northeast Texas. It is an honor to meet your Excellency. It is good to see you again, Colonel Ahumada."

"It is always good to see a friend and distinguished citizen of Mexico, Colonel Turner," replied Ahumada.

I could feel many sets of eyes at my back as I was addressed as Colonel. I had deliberately not mentioned my promotion. "Your Excellency. Colonel Ahumada. May I present the militia of Navasota Crossing?"

At that signal, the assembled men and boys snapped to attention and shouldered their weapons. As our settlement had grown, sixty-three members of the militia stood in home spun woolens, buckskins, and store bought clothes. They didn't look like much compared to Teran's lancers, but they were crack shots with their rifles and they knew their business. We had prepared a little demonstration for our illustrious visitors.

"With you Excellency's permission, my men will perform a rifle drill."

"Yes, Colonel Turner. You intrigue me."

"Assume your positions for rifle drill!"

The men broke into three ranks facing east. We had placed twenty stiffly dried deer skins fastened to posts one hundred yards away. "Alternate volley fire by ranks! Front rank. Ready. Aim. Fire!" Every other man in the front rank fired an aimed shot, immediately followed by the other half of the line.

"Rear rank advance. Ready. Aim. Fire!" They advanced beyond the front rank and fired an alternate volley as had the front rank. "Rear rank advance. Ready. Aim. Fire!" They, too, advanced beyond the current front rank and fired an alternate volley. "Halt!" The deer skins hung in tatters.

Beyond them at two hundred and fifty yards was another set of deer skins. "Assume skirmish formation." The men spread out and lay down propped up on their elbows about six feet from the men on either side of him in a long staggered line. "Commence firing!" Every third man fired an aimed shot, then reloaded while the others continued the staggered fire. The first men who shot were now ready to fire again. This kept up a sustained fire for several minutes. After the men had completed two cycles, I ordered them to stop.

There was a murmur from the Mexican troops. Even from this distance it was possible to see the large number of holes in the deer skins. Colonel Ahumada rode out and inspected the targets.

"Colonel Turner, even the farthest targets are riddled with holes. This is excellent marksmanship."

"Sir, there is one final demonstration." Tanner, Gray and Logan rode out to place three clay pots turned upside down on posts at four hundred yards. "Chance, Nick, Cody. Show the gentlemen what you can do."

They knelt on the ground and took careful aim. Chance assumed command. "On my order. Ready. Aim. Fire!" All three pots exploded with the direct hits.

Applause burst out from the Mexican soldiers and our militia. "Company dismissed!" The men smiled because they knew they had done well. They gathered their gear and gradually returned to their work.

Teran smiled from his black horse. "The enemies of Mexico have much to fear from your company. You are to be commended for your training."

My friend from the defeat of the Fredonian Rebellion, Colonel Ahumada, grinned widely. "You did very well, Colonel."

We had borrowed the Applewhite's large tent to entertain our guests. It had been set up in the meadow south of the settlement. Refreshments were provided for the entire delegation. The soldiers set up their camp near the tent.

The Mexican troops tended their animals and settled in for the night. Several of us stayed up late and visited with Teran and his staff. They had endless questions and we tried to provide accurate answers. They had noticed the good repair of the road and the neatness of our community and fields. In the morning, we would take a riding tour of the area.

We rode south to show off the brick, tile and pottery works, plus the tannery and saddle shop. There were several good farms in that part of the settlement. We then headed north. Teran admired the productivity of our farms and the quality of our livestock.

"What is this crop, Colonel Turner? I am not familiar with it."

"Sir, that is what is known as ribbon cane or sweet sorghum. We use it to make a syrup very much like molasses."

The livestock caught his attention. "These are some of the finest mules I have ever seen. These cattle are not of the common type found in Texas. They are of obvious quality. Your horses are remarkable. They are taller and more muscular than the native horses."

"Your Excellency is very kind. The credit is due to our fine Shorthorn bull, Thoroughbred stallion and Spanish jack."

I signaled to Lucius, who rode up leading another horse. It was a beautiful blood bay stallion with a black mane and tail. The only white on him was a single white star on his forehead. His dark eyes shone with intelligence.

The entire mounted party dismounted to admire him. I had Lucius move the saddle from his own horse to the bay.

The bay spun right and left on command and backed up with ease. Lucius took him through his paces there in the meadow. He had a smooth, ground eating trot and a beautiful lope.

"Your Excellency, this stallion is only two years old, but already well grown and adequately trained. He is called *Estrello de Tejas*, the Star of Texas. I have selected him from my own herd as an humble gift for you."

A collective gasp could be heard from Teran's entourage. Teran had his aide move the saddle from the magnificent black horse he was riding to the bay. He sprang into the saddle like a cavalry trooper and put the young horse through his paces.

"Colonel Turner, you do me great honor with your gift. A horse such as this is rare indeed, even among the greatest haciendas of Mexico. I accept him with much gratitude."

On our ride back to the settlement, Nick asked "Colonel, are you crazy giving that stud horse to that Mexican fella? That horse must be worth better than three hundred pesos."

I smiled at Nick. "It never hurts to buy a little good will when you can. Besides, I've got three other young studs better than that hid out in the river bottoms. You can never be too careful, either."

That night, we prepared a feast for Teran, his entire escort and the whole community. Beef had been slowly roasted over oak fires to tender perfection. Dried beans had been cooked with salt pork. Countless pans of corn bread had been baked to be served with fresh butter. Cobblers made from dried fruit lined the groaning tables of food. Every one ate until they could eat no more.

After our meal, various musicians tuned their fiddles, guitars and banjos to entertain the crowd. There were musicians among our Mexican guests, too, who played the guitar for us. It was a memorable evening for all of us.

Before Teran's departure the following morning, mounted on his new horse, he commended the industry of our settlement, the quality of our crops and livestock, and the capability of our militia. Colonel Ahumada shook my hand. "Colonel Turner, you continue to amaze me. I am proud to call you friend. You have made a positive impression on his Excellency. I have seen his written assessment of your situation here, and it is favorable. He wrote that if all of Texas was as your community, the northern boundaries of Mexico would be strong, safe and prosperous."

8

Fall, 1829, Navasota Crossing, Austin's Colony, Texas

OUR CORN WAS RIPE and harvest was in full swing in September of 1829, when the alarm bell sounded. The lookout in the bell tower shouted that he could see a cloud of dust coming from the north. Every one abandoned their field work and hurriedly began moving their most valuable animals to safety. We all knew there were no white settlers to our north, only Indians.

Chance rode north to investigate, as the rest of us prepared for an attack. Some sought shelter at the fort, while others manned the building of the settlement one hundred yards to the south. The school children were seen safely to their families. The militia quickly assembled in front of the gate of the fort awaiting orders.

The lookout hailed us again. "Colonel Turner, I see riders now; three Indians riding together and coming fast. Chance is with them."

In minutes they were at the fort. Gray Feather, our Wichita friend, had sent three trusted young braves to find me. I spoke quite a bit of Wichita, but the words of the young spokesman tumbled out so fast I only caught bits and pieces. "Chance, what's he saying?"

"Looks like some Wichita braves stole horses from a Cherokee village on the Trinity. Their village complained to Duwali, High Chief of the Cherokee. He is leading a Cherokee war band of over a hundred warriors to attack Gray Feather's village up on the Brazos. The Wichita sent riders to meet Duwali to parley with them, but he killed them. Gray Feather wants your help and needs it fast."

"We haven't ever had any trouble with the Cherokee, but we don't know them like we do the Wichita. They have been our friends since we came here exploring in 1817. Gray Feather and his braves risked their lives to keep us from being killed by the Comanche. We owe them. We're liable to get in the middle of a big mess if we try to take on a hundred Cherokee. They are pretty salty fighters. Maybe we can negotiate a truce."

"Cody, you take relay horses and ride hard to Louisiana Landing. Tell Captain Rob to leave enough men to protect their settlement and load the rest on his steamboat. He is to head up the Brazos as fast as he can to the Wichita village. You come up the river with him.

"Chance, you are coming with me. Pick out twenty good men and get ready to travel. "Richard Moore, you'll be in charge here at the fort until we get back."

"Marcus, get these Wichita some food and water. Trade them for some fresh horses. We are leaving in fifteen minutes."

Cody left in a cloud of dust. He was riding a fast horse and leading three more. He should make it in six or seven hard hours riding to Louisiana Landing.

Our group consisted of twenty well-mounted militia, Chance, the three Wichita and me. We headed straight north, letting the Wichita braves lead us. Gray Feather's village was on the east bank of the Brazos about thirty miles to the northwest.

We forded the Navasota at an unnamed crossing and struck out cross country for the Wichita camp. We stopped only long enough to water and rest the horses. We rode on into the night, following game trails familiar to the scouts. In most places we had to ride single file and dodge overhanging branches. As we drew closer to the camp, we could hear scattered gunfire and see flames reflected in the night sky.

When we were within half a mile of the Wichita camp the scouts slipped ahead on foot to evaluate the situation. The rest of us moved a little farther west so that we would have the Brazos at our backs, then proceeded north along the bank toward the camp. We settled down waiting for the scouts' report. We didn't light a fire or do anything to reveal our presence.

It was about two hours until they returned. Their faces revealed much of the story; Chance translated the rest.

"Major, I mean, Colonel, things are bad for the Wichita. There are over a hundred Cherokee with rifles. They are pressing the village in a semicircle back toward the river. There are about sixty Wichita braves fighting from inside the camp. They have sent riders out to ask for help from the Caddo, Tonkawa and other Wichita bands. They have a palisade around the perimeter which is helping to hold the Cherokee out for now. They can't last long the way things look."

"How well are the Wichita armed?"

"A few rifles, lots of muskets, bows and arrows. They have their horse herd inside the palisade."

"How about the Cherokee? Rifles or muskets? Where is Duwali's camp?"

"Mostly they have rifled muskets. They don't know for sure where Duwali has his war camp. The Cherokee horse herd is east of the village under heavy guard. Gray Feather will send more news at dawn."

"Colonel, I do remember how Gray Feather and his warriors saved our backsides in that fight with the Comanche the first time we came to Texas."

"How could any of us ever forget it?"

"These Wichita have been our friends for a long time. I can't sit by and watch them get slaughtered."

"I know, Chance. I feel the same way. I want to try to broker some kind of peace talks, but if it comes to it, we join sides with the Wichita. I hope Rob gets here soon with extra men. We are in a bad spot right now."

The lights of the river boat twinkled in the pre-dawn grayness as it quietly pushed against the current of the muddy Brazos. We signaled them with a small torch waved from the bank. The pilot house blinked a night lantern in response. They pulled within voice range and set an anchor at the bow waiting for instructions.

Gray Feather sent another messenger. He expected a small reinforcement of Wichita from another band. He also expected a band of Tonkawa to arrive from the north at any time. The Caddo had declined to send help, as they lived nearest the Cherokee and must maintain peace with them. He asked us to attack from the river's edge behind the Cherokee line and try to turn their flank.

I send word to Rob to move the *Brazos Belle* behind the Wichita camp and to pour rifle fire from the upper deck into the Cherokee who were attacking from the north. They were to keep the river boat far enough out in the river to avoid being boarded by the Cherokee. We moved north along the bank leaving our horses behind, hobbled and on a picket line.

As we attacked, the Wichita inside the palisade poured all they had into the Cherokee. They were caught by surprise and immediately began to retreat toward the front of the camp.

As the river boat drew even with us, the fourteen militia men on her upper deck rained lead rifle balls into the retreating Cherokee. They steamed on until they were even with the north side of the camp. The Wichita and Tonkawa reinforcements had arrived and emerged from the forest as the riflemen from the river boat continued a hot fire. The Cherokee retreated toward the front of the camp.

Soon the whole body of Cherokee warriors was forced to the front of the village. They were making a well organized fighting retreat to the east. The Tonkawa fought with a ferocity I had seldom seen. They attacked the Cherokee like wolves among sheep. The Cherokee were finally successful in extricating themselves from the fight.

Gray Feather, Chance and I appeared before the Wichita village holding our rifles horizontal above our heads in a signal that was equivalent to a flag of truce. Duwali and two of his sub-chiefs advanced making the same sign. Gray Feather introduced me as the Chief of the white men east of the Brazos. Through Chance, I asked if we could sit, smoke and talk. Duwali agreed.

We moved to the shade of a large live oak tree. Both Wichita and Cherokee pipes were lit and passed among us. Duwali and Gray Feather both spoke good Spanish, so we were all able to communicate well.

"Duwali, why has the High Chief of the Cherokee come so far west to make war against my friend and brother, Gray Feather?"

"Their young men come to steal our horses. I warn them, but they keep stealing."

"Gray Feather, is this true?"

"The young men always steal horses. I do not know where they get them."

"Duwali, is it not the way of young men to steal horses back and forth?"

"My young men are successful farmers and hunters. They trade for their horses and leave our neighbors alone."

"So they never steal from the Caddo, Tonkawa, or Wichita?"

"They only take back what is rightfully theirs."

"Chief Duwali, are there Wichita horses among your war ponies? Gray Feather, are there Cherokee horses in your camp?" Both chiefs sat in silence.

"Would you agree to allow me to inspect your herds with each of you and restore the horses to their owners?" They reluctantly nodded in agreement. Both ordered their warriors and allies to stand down.

I positioned my men between the two warring groups. It was not a pleasant place to be. Rob's twenty well armed men still had all of us within rifle range from the upper deck of the steamboat. Their presence exerted a calming, sobering effect on the combatants.

After inspection, a dozen Cherokee horses were led out of the Wichita village. Four Wichita horses were found in the Cherokee herd. There was also a Tonkawa horse in the Cherokee band, as well as one of ours with the Wichita, much to Gray Feather's embarrassment. It seemed there was enough guilt to go around.

At this point, I assumed the mantle of authority given to me by the government of Mexico. I told the Cherokee they must no longer raid from the Wichita and that the Wichita must no longer steal from the Cherokee. If another conflict occurred, I would send for Mexican soldiers to intervene. The Mexicans would not be as patient as I had been, and they would kill their women and children and burn their villages. If they would keep the peace for one year, they could come to my settlement and receive gifts for honoring their pledge of peace. We sat and smoked. It was agreed.

The Cherokee left that day. We stayed to make sure they did not return, although I sensed Duwali was a man of his word. Rob, with the Upper Brazos militia, returned to Louisiana Landing while we retraced our steps to Navasota Crossing. It was not the last time we would hear of Duwali or the Cherokee.

⑨

Winter 1829, Navasota Landing, Austin's Colony, Texas

NANCY AND I FOUND ourselves somewhat cramped in our cabin with five children, three of whom were teenagers. We didn't want to leave the safety of the fort, so decided to build a new cabin on the same spot.

The boys used the wagon to haul rocks from the river and stockpiled them near the construction site. I had the pottery works fire enough tile to completely roof the new cabin. It would last forever and was fireproof and unaffected by hail smaller than cannon balls.

I sent in a special order for glass windows with Captain Rob. He could get them along the coast shipped in from New Orleans.

We carefully laid out the foundation forty feet long and twenty feet wide. It was to be two stories tall with a wide front porch and a second story gallery. The house would face the south and still be the southwest corner of the fort. The fireplaces were to be of brick from the pottery works. There would be one on both the east and west ends of the house, both upstairs and down.

We dug a trench for the foundation which we filled with small stones, sand and gravel mixed with burned lime and water. When it cured, it was hard as brick. The raised part of the foundation was made of carefully selected and fitted stones joined together with burned lime and sand.

Nancy had lived in a rough frontier cabin long enough. We fitted a saw blade to our mule powered mill, using a special gear to increase the speed of the saw blade. We would use sawed lumber for the house. Cypress beams were used for the floor joists. Cypress wouldn't rot like other wood. We cut thick pine boards for the floor, which the carpenter planed smooth for us. We also used them for the interior walls and stairs.

As the walls went up, the window openings were framed with cypress, and the double-hung windows carefully fitted into place. We had glass in all the windows, including upstairs. They could be opened at the top or the bottom to let air flow through the house.

Heavy oak shutters were anchored to cover the windows, with heavy locking oak bars. Each set of shutters fit together to form a gun port where they joined. Both the front and back doors were made of very heavy oak, and fitted with iron straps and hinges. Each door had a small opening hinged into it at the right height and size for a gun port. Next to each door and window, we built gun racks.

The interior walls were plastered smooth over the planks and painted white. The floors were given a final sanding, then rubbed with a mixture of boiled linseed oil and turpentine until they had a soft glow.

We hired Mr. Morgan to build us a table and chairs for eight, plus new bed frames and dressers for each of the bedrooms. I surprised Nancy and the girls with oval mirrors from New Orleans for their walls.

When we were finished, the old cabin was taken down and reassembled by one of the new families across the road. We adjusted the palisade to tie into the new house, which was by no means a cabin.

"Aaron, it is the grandest thing I could have ever imagined."

"You deserve it, Nancy, and a whole lot more besides." I picked her up and carried her across the threshold into one of the finest homes east of the Brazos.

Lucius and Marcus had a room together, as did both the girls. The little ones shared a room, and Nancy and I, after all these years, finally had a room of our own. She had the four poster bed fitted out in a fine quilt, feather pillows, a cotton-stuffed mattress and cotton sheets. She kept her brush and comb on the dresser in front of the mirror. Except for the loaded guns in the rack by the window, you might have thought we were in a fine home back in Georgia or South Carolina.

We were so happy with our new house. We loved to sit on the front porch or the upstairs gallery and enjoy the sunset together. This seemed to be the pinnacle of successful comfort and reward for all of our hard work.

After planting season, just as we were harvesting the oats and wheat, Tanner Moore rode out to the field where I was working.

"Afternoon, Reverend Turner."

"Evenin', Tanner. What brings you out this way and away from your work?"

"I wasn't having that much fun working. Pa sent me out here to let you know Captain Rob is at the settlement asking for you."

I told Marcus and Lucius to keep working as I laid my scythe against the rail fence. I saddled the horse I had left tied in the shade and rode back with Tanner. As I approached the settlement, I heard, and then saw Rob entertaining a small group of listeners on the front porch of the trading post. "Ahoy, Captain Rob! Hope you ain't worn your jaws out and hurt these good folks' ears with all your tall tales."

"Ahoy, yourself, you old farmer, soldier, preacher, Indian fighter and scalawag. Let's go up to your house and talk a while."

We unsaddled the horses and turned them into a stall near the house with some grass hay and a little oats. We walked in through the back door of the house. Nancy had seen us coming.

"Lord, Captain Rob! You are a sight for sore eyes. Let me show you the new house."

"I'm following you, Nancy. A fellow could get lost in a house this big."

"After a brief tour of the house, she sent one of the children out to draw up a jug of hard cider from the well. "I'll have supper on in a little while. You and Aaron sit and visit. I'm not taking 'No' for an answer."

"I would never presume to argue with the lady of such a fine home."

When Nancy left the room, his face became deadly serious. He reached in his pocket as he pulled out a pouch. "I brought you a copy of the newspaper and a letter from Stephen Austin."

Lieutenant Colonel Aaron Turner
Alcalde, Northeast District, Austin's Colony, Texas

My dear friend,

I regret that I am unable to attend to you personally. I have sent this letter under the hand of Captain Contois. You will find a copy of the *Texas Gazette* published here in San Felipe. It contains an edited version of changes in Mexican law which may have a direct effect on our colony.

I am afraid that it may have an adverse effect on further Anglo colonization from the United States into Texas. The newspaper article has withheld, at my specific request, certain inflammatory parts of the new law. I pray that the law will be amended quickly before it incites our colonists.

I am enclosing an unedited summary for you to read and share with Captain Contois in his capacity as

Alcalde of the Upper Brazos District. Do not allow the unedited summary to circulate, or be read by any persons other than yourself. You may circulate the *Gazette* as you see fit.

I will be available should you have any questions or concerns. I plan to contact you as soon as certain issues are resolved.

Sincerely,
Colonel Stephen F. Austin
Empresario, Austin's Colony, Texas

The summary he attached riveted my attention and sent shivers down my spine. I felt a cold hand squeeze my heart as I read the new law. Rob and I saw immediately why it so concerned Austin.

Law of April Sixth, 1830, Summary

Gentlemen, these are the problem areas of which I am most concerned.

There shall be no more Anglo-American colonization in Texas effective immediately. Non-American immigrants will be welcomed.

Slavery, in all its forms, is abolished in the entire Republic of Mexico effective immediately. Existing slaves are to be freed and no new slaves shall be brought into any part of Mexico.

No new colonies shall be established. Existing colonies shall be allowed to continue to function, but colonists not already under contract to settle shall be turned back. Any unfilled quotas or unclaimed land in any of the existing colonies shall be forfeit to the Republic of Mexico.

I whistled as I read the summary. "Rob, this is worse than unfriendly, it is downright nasty. I liked that fellow Teran well enough. I guess he figures the American colonists are getting too big for their britches."

"I can tell you this, Aaron. Our friends Applewhite and Groce would be ready to start a shooting war if anybody tries to free their slaves. Groce has over a hundred slaves himself, and Applewhite has nearly thirty counting kids."

We finished our wheat and oats harvest, and spent the summer cultivating our corn, cotton and food crops. I had started using a two-row cultivator drawn by a pair of horses or mules. I could cover many times as many acres in a day as a good man with a hoe. It worked well until the crops were over knee high. At that point, if weeds were still a problem, we resorted to hand hoeing. Our vegetable plot had to be hand hoed anyway. As the corn and cotton grew big enough, they shaded the middles and kept the weeds down.

Settlers continued to trundle down the Camino Real on foot, horseback and by wagon, but now the pace of immigration had again increased. Many of them carried certificates of settlement in Austin's Colony with their names written in the blanks and signed by Stephen Austin. These certificates were being distributed in New Orleans, Natchitoches, and Galveston by his agents. When they arrived at San Felipe, one of Austin's deputies assigned them a tract of land. This effectively skirted the letter and the intent of the new law.

Rob brought news that Secretary Teran had ordered the establishment of a new town called Anahuac at the mouth of the Trinity on upper Galveston Bay. Anahuac was an old Aztec word for "by the water" or "troubled water." It looked like it was going to be nothing but trouble.

All coastal shipping was to be cleared through customs for

import and export duties at Anahuac, regardless of what Texas port to which it was destined. It would mean a hundred extra miles of sailing across Galveston Bay to pay taxes nobody wanted to pay.

"Now we have export taxes on cotton and import taxes on plows. Nearly everything we get comes up river now. Folks around here aren't going to like this, Rob."

"No they ain't. Especially since Teran had 'em build a fort there to back it up. They've already got the garrison installed. Teran appointed a hot-headed no-good from Kentucky named John Bradburn as commander at the fort. He even changed his name to Juan Bradburn so he would sound more Mexican."

"I can tell you one more thing, too, Aaron. Just since they started taxing goods at Anahuac, there is plenty more stuff being sent over land down the Camino Real to avoid the taxes. It is too expensive to move cotton that way, but there are plenty of high value imports coming into Texas untaxed. The ships that load their cotton at Brazosport don't find it convenient to stop at Anahuac. They take the longer route outside of Galveston Island and kind of forget to pay the customs. Ol' Colonel Bradburn wants a whole fleet of revenue cutters to enforce the taxes. I brought you a letter from Stephen Austin. I nearly forgot."

Lieutenant Colonel Aaron Turner,
Alcalde, Northeast District, Austin's Colony

Lieutenant Colonel Turner,

I trust you and your family are well. I will get straight to the point.

President Guerrero has exempted Texas from the slavery clause in the Law of April 6, 1830.

I have issued certificates of settlement at points of entry into Texas for our colony. I suspect you have seen some of them by now.

I do not like the situation at Anahuac. That fool Bradburn is spoiling for an armed conflict.

I was unable to resolve the customs issue.

I have been elected to serve as the representative from Texas to the State Legislature of Tejas y Coahuila in Monclova. Perhaps more can be done there.

Sincerely,
Stephen Austin

We did not have to provide gifts to the Wichita and Cherokee. The young Wichita braves continued to steal Cherokee horses. The Cherokee retaliated with a lightning raid against the Wichita village on the Brazos. Caught unprepared, the Wichita were soundly defeated with heavy losses. After the fight, the remaining Wichita moved their village far up the Brazos to the northwest.

That fall, we rafted an even larger crop of cotton down the Navasota as far as Groce's plantation, then by steamboat to Brazosport. We discovered it was less work to load a single stack of bales and use more rafts. Stacking them higher was too much work and more likely to snag over-hanging limbs.

It sold untaxed at a good price to a buyer for a cotton mill in North Carolina. We were openly defying the law. Our justification was that it was an unfair, bad law. That made ignoring it permissible in our own minds.

As the waves washed against the pier, they carried a message of discontent and danger to Texas' shores. The sea foam hissed into the sand and the wind from the Gulf whispered of evil days to come.

10

Spring 1831, San Felipe, Austin's Colony, Texas

IN THE SPRING OF 1831, Marcus, Lucius and I made a trip down the Brazos with Captain Rob to pick up supplies for the settlement. We left a heavy wagon and a good team of mules at Louisiana Landing for our return trip. We stopped at San Felipe for me to file some reports with Stephen Austin in connection with my role as alcalde and commander of the militia.

"Well, Colonel Turner, I am pleased with your reports. Your militia is obviously well trained and a unit we can trust in a time of need. The progress of settlement in your district is going well, especially at Navasota Crossing. Your community is as self-supporting as any in Texas. You are adding acres of cotton as a cash crop, too."

"Captain Contois, your settlement at Louisiana Landing is growing and prospering. I am amazed at the cotton production from the Brazos River bottom land. Your steamboat has helped the prosperity of the entire Brazos valley. So far, I have not received any negative comment about your decision to arm slaves and include them in the militia. However, I have made it a point to conceal it from Mr. Groce."

"Colonel Austin, when the Comanche come calling, ten extra men with rifles can make a huge difference. Those rifles don't know if the men pulling the triggers are black or white."

"I agree with you completely, Captain. Even so, Jared Groce would not approve, I think."

"Colonel Austin, he knows. Remember, he is my father-in-law. There ain't much gets by that man. He chewed on me pretty good about it. I think if the Comanche get to raiding as far south as his place, he may have a change of heart."

We all laughed. Rob had a unique way of summarizing things.

Austin rose and motioned us into the next room. "I have people I would like for you to meet. Gentlemen, this is Father Michael Muldoon. He has been appointed Curate for all the Catholic churches in the Texas colonies."

Before I could see it coming, a bear sized man grabbed me in a tight embrace. "It's proud to meet you, I am, Colonel Turner!" In turn, he also squeezed the life out of Rob, Lucius and Marcus. "These are fine strapping sons, Aaron. Are ye lads married or happy?" He roared laughing at his own joke. "I suspect ye are still prowling about for the right lass."

The boys just smiled red-faced in reply.

"And Captain Rob, I hear you have the finest steamboat on the Brazos and a beautiful young wife. It is proud to meet you, I am. Do you have a house full of children yet like a good Catholic?"

"We're still practicing until we get it right, Father."

We didn't know what to make of Father Muldoon, but it was hard not to like him. His round face, sparkling blue eyes and red hair reminded me of my Irish heritage.

Rob never missed the opportunity for mischief. "And do you have a fine house full of children, Father?'

Colonel Austin gasped in horror, as my sons giggled. "No. There's none that I know of, Rob. Why do you think I left Ireland in such a hurry? I have always been tempted to become Anglican so I can raise a crop." His good humor relieved all of us.

Austin then called to his assistant who brought in two more guests. "This is my sister's son, Moses Austin Bryan. He is thirteen and is to be my personal assistant."

We exchanged greetings. Moses was tall and well-built for his age. There was a definite resemblance to his uncle. He seemed genuinely glad to meet us, and we took an immediate liking to the young man.

"May I also introduce my first cousin, Henry Austin? He has been a sailing master on the high seas and a river pilot on the Mississippi and Red rivers. He has come to Texas to seek his fortune. He has bought land down on the lower Brazos with the intention of founding a cotton plantation. He has named it Bolivar Plantation."

Henry Austin was cordial enough, but did not possess Stephen's easy grace and polished manners. The set of his jaw suggested to me he could be a hard man. He looked like he had been eating green persimmons.

"Captain Contois, I will be imposing on you to take Henry, Moses and Father Muldoon down river as far as Bolivar Plantation. Henry is anxious to begin building his fortune. Moses and Father Muldoon will be continuing on a tour of the settlements along the Brazos. They would like to accompany you down to the coast and back as far as Louisiana Landing."

We enjoyed the company of young Moses and Father Muldoon a great deal, but I must admit we were not sad to see the brooding Henry step ashore. Our Curate was full of questions about the colony and the colonists. He was always in a fine mood and loved to tell stories and jokes. Moses soaked in everything he saw and asked a stream of thoughtful questions. I could see that for one so young, he would prove a great asset to his uncle.

On our arrival at Louisiana Landing, Father Muldoon and Moses toured the Applewhite's plantation and the smaller, but no less successful, farms of the Lane brothers. He convened a special mass that night at the Applewhite's home. I thought Mr. Applewhite was going to die of a fit! Rob and I exchanged quick grins.

"Now I can be seeing that you are all good Catholics, but some of you have had only a civil marriage by Colonel Turner in his capacity as the alcalde. Rather than do a marriage rite for each couple, I will simply sign in the records of the Holy Church that as Curate I declare you all to be married in the eyes of the Church."

We all breathed a silent sigh of relief. "Now, as to the childrens' baptisms, Aaron, I assume you have kept accurate records?"

"Well, um, yes, Father."

"I'm guessing that these children have already been baptized?"

"Well, um, yes, Father. In my capacity as alcalde, and lacking a priest, I felt it important to administer the necessary rites."

"Grand! I will simply initial the birth and baptismal records to show they are all good little Catholics. Oh, and Aaron, I am allowed to appoint lay members to act on my behalf in the absence of a priest. I assume you will have no difficulty continuing to do marriages, baptisms and funerals?"

My face reddened as I realized he had used the word "continuing." It seems nothing had escaped the attention of those twinkling blue eyes. "Oh, Aaron, in case you were wondering, my counterpart in the Diocese of Georgia checked with the state ministerial licensing board. It seems there is an ordained Methodist minister by the name of Aaron Turner. That would be you, wouldn't it lad?"

I was caught in my own trap. My stomach was in a knot and my heart was in my throat. My mouth was so dry I could barely speak. I looked into his face for some sign of what was coming. I could be expelled from Texas or even imprisoned. He sensed my anxiety, and smiled broadly, putting a hand on my shoulder. "Yes, Father Muldoon. I am the same man."

"Well, my lad, isn't it magnificent that the Holy church has converted a Protestant minister?" With that he slapped my back and gave me a big grin and a wink.

"Why, yes it is, Father Muldoon; rather amazing don't you think?"

"Would you mind taking the evening air with me?"

Once outside, he explained his position to me. "Aaron, please be calling me Michael in person, for I consider ye a friend. Do you think I did not know ye were a Methodist minister and almost all the settlers are Protestant? You are tending to their spiritual needs. I have no one else to send. As long as their names appear on the Holy Church rolls and they live Godly lives, my Archbishop and the Mexican authorities will be content. They will be good 'Muldoon Catholics.' You most certainly may keep ministering to the people as you always have done, discretely."

Relief flooded through me. "Thank you, Michael. You will find me a most diligent, and discrete, 'Muldoon Catholic'."

After supper, Lucius and Marcus invited Moses Austin to join them in a snipe hunt. They led him out into the trees along the banks of the Brazos just as the fireflies were making their appearance. They positioned him along a game trail in the trees holding a burlap sack. He was to yell out "Whoop, snipe!" every few minutes and nab the elusive non-flying bird as he ran down the trail. Lucius and Marcus told him they would walk east a ways and drive the snipe back toward him.

They snickered at their deceit as they trotted out of the woods. They laughed out loud as they heard Moses yell "Whoop, snipe!" Soon the woods grew silent, so they headed back to the Applewhite's cabin.

When they arrived, they discovered Moses sitting on the front porch holding the empty sack. "We hunt snipe back in Missouri, too!" They all had a good laugh together.

When the boys and I returned home, we found a group of settlers camped south of the settlement. The group was formed of closely related members of one family and a handful of friends. They were heading to settle to the northwest of us across the Navasota and halfway to the Brazos. Most of them were named Parker, or were related to the Parkers by marriage, including a family named Adamson.

The Adamson family had three sons, Brian, Kevin and Parker. They were seventeen, twelve and eleven. Both of their parents were teachers who hoped to take up land there and also begin a school. Tanner, Logan and Gray became fast friends with the younger two. My stepson, Marcus, became good friends with Brian.

The Parkers were the first settlers we knew of heading that direction. Dangerously, their settlement would be directly in one of the favored war paths of the Comanche. But Mr. Parker indicated that they planned to build a stout fort. I told him I was commander of the militias in that part of the colony. If they needed help getting their militia organized, or if they needed assistance, they could send a fast rider to find me.

In their party was a family named Smith, who had come down the Mississippi on a flat boat as far as the Red River, then overland to settle with the Parkers. They had two beautiful daughters who caught the attention of Lucius and Marcus. The boys were twenty-one and eighteen, and each had already received their own land grants. The girls were Ilene, eighteen, and Glynna, sixteen. Just as the bluebonnets and Indian paint brushes were blooming in the meadow, so was young love flowering in our home. Before the travelers' continued their trip, I was asked to perform a double wedding.

This was service I was proud to perform, as I considered both boys my own sons. We held a brief, pretty little wedding ceremony in the spring sunshine. We enjoyed a special feast that lasted well into the night.

As Nancy and I finally got ready for bed, I heard her giggling. "What is so funny?"

"Aaron, do you think we might be grandparents in a year or two?"

"Those kids all looked pretty healthy to me. I'd be kind of

disappointed if we don't have some grandkids by then. Why do you ask?"

"Then we'll have grandchildren and a child pretty near the same age."

My male mind was slow to unravel the message. I rolled over and pulled the covers up over my shoulders. Then it hit me. I was ecstatic! "Nancy, when are you due?"

"Right around Christmas, I think."

"Well, I guess I got the spring planting done right on time," I laughed. I held her close to me all night in the bed in the house we had built on the land we had wrestled from the wilderness. In all of this, I could see God's hand of blessing. With a prayer of thanks on my mind, I drifted off to a peaceful sleep.

Nancy gave birth in December to our sweet daughter, Francis. She was the bright star of our Christmas that year. Our harvest had filled the corn cribs, cellars, hay lofts and smoke houses. We had gradually increased our cotton acres and enjoyed a good crop. As soon as it was ginned, we loaded it on three rafts and floated it down the Navasota on the day after Christmas. We met Captain Rob at Groce's plantation two days later and arrived in Brazosport the next day.

Secretary Teran, now most often called General Teran, had suspected too much cotton was leaving the Brazos River untaxed and failing to report at Anahuac on the Trinity as ordered. In response, he had a fort built at Velasco near the mouth of the Brazos. It was armed with cannon and one hundred and seventy Mexican soldiers. Many of the sailing ships and steamboats quietly ignored the customs dock at the fort.

On December 31, 1831,as we watched from the pilot house of our steamboat, and much to the amazement of everyone, the soldiers in the fort fired across the bow of a group of three small sailing ships which had failed to stop at the customs dock.

The ships were only lightly armed, but they returned fire with a few four pounder cannon and swivel guns. The action ended as the ships sailed past the reach of the fort's guns. No sailors were harmed and only one Mexican soldier had suffered minor injuries.

The unthinkable had happened. Shots had been exchanged in anger between Mexican soldiers and Anglo citizens of Texas. We were all citizens of the Republic of Mexico, sworn to uphold the constitution, although that seemed to be a moving target. Many of us had taken up arms in support and defense of Mexico.

As alcalde of the northeast district of Austin's Colony, I was a duly appointed official of the government of Mexico. As a Lieutenant Colonel in the militia, I had a direct allegiance to the Mexican army.

I had always thought the new tariffs unfair, and the new constitution seemed strongly biased against Anglo-American citizens of Texas. But armed conflict with the government of Mexico was unthinkable. However, I saw nothing unethical about avoiding an unfair tax. My family had known how to skirt unfair taxes for generations. I found myself very undecided about the whole ordeal.

But one thing was clear, the Mexican government meant business. I would not be able to sit on the fence for long. I feared that there were dark, dangerous days before us.

11

Spring 1832, Gulf coast of Texas, between the
mouths of the Trinity and Brazos Rivers

CIVIL WAR BROKE OUT
in Mexico. The type of war that turns a country inside
out, destroys the economy and grinds the people into
dust. The type of war that stains the soil with the blood of
soldiers and citizens and fouls the water with the bodies
of the innocent. And in civil war, as in any other, it was
the poor who suffered the most.

There had long been two main political points of
view in Mexico. The federalist point of view supported a
decentralized government, power to the individual states
and only a minimal central government.

The centralist philosophy supported a concentration
of power at the national level at the expense of the
individual states. The United States was a good example
of a federalist type of government in 1832.

President Bustamonte of Mexico was a strong
centralist. One of his primary supporters was General
Manuel y Mier de Teran, who had visited our community
not so long ago.

The champion of the federalist cause was General
Antonio de Lopez de Santa Anna. He and I had been well

acquainted in years gone by. Now armies backing those two factions were locked in a fierce and bloody conflict for the control and destiny of Mexico.

Most Texans hoped Santa Anna would prevail. We were comfortable with the politics of federalism. We wanted to see Texas become an independent state within Mexico, no longer tied to Coahuila. In Texas, the government was dominated by centralists appointed by Bustamonte, so the government supported the status quo. Not a one among us felt free to express our political views where they could be known to the government.

Colonel Juan Bradford, a rabid supporter of Bustamonte, flexed his quarrelsome muscles. The small community of Liberty had sprung up near Anahuac. The citizens' federalist leanings were well known. Bradford had declared the town an illegal settlement and forcefully dissolved their town council. Any slaves in or near the community were declared free. A strict interpretation of Mexican law made it illegal for non-native Mexicans to serve as attorneys, even though the practice had been quietly allowed for years. Bradford arrested all the Anglo attorneys in Liberty and Anahuac and other "traitors." He had them jailed promptly without a trial. Among the imprisoned Anglo-Texans was a fiery young attorney, William B. Travis. Bradford's actions in Anahuac on the Trinity River precipitated what would become known as the "Battle of Velasco" miles away on the Brazos.

A party of colonists, offended by what had happened at Anahuac, took up arms in response and assembled near the detested customs collection fort at Velasco. The Mexican fortress was under the command of Lieutenant Colonel Domingo de Ugartecha. The fort was built of a double palisade of strong logs, with the rows set six feet apart. The space between the rows of logs was packed with rubble. The walls were defended by one hundred and seventy Mexican soldiers supported by several four and six pounder cannon.

The rebellious colonists knew they could not take the fort without help. John Austin, who as I far as I knew was of no relation to Stephen Austin, arrived with a contingent of volunteers and a six pounder cannon. His party set out to attack the fort from the land.

William Russell commanded an armed schooner, the *Brazoria*, which mounted three small cannon. On June 26, 1832, the Texans mounted a combined land and sea assault against the Mexican fort. The Mexicans fought back furiously.

The design of the Mexican fort was excellent to stop sea borne cannon balls. But for soldiers to return fire at a land based foe, they had to fire from the exposed top of the walls. There were no rifle ports where they could shoot from relative safety.

The Mexicans also were armed with escopetas. These large smooth bore muskets were ineffective beyond about seventy yards. The Texans, for the most part, were armed with rifled muskets like we carried, that were accurate to four hundred yards in experienced hands. They were slower to reload than the escopetas, but their accuracy more than compensated for this small disadvantage.

Round shot from all four cannon poured into the fort. Although the round shot did minimal damage to the stout palisades, they were quite deadly to the men on top of the walls. The combined effect of the rifles and cannon was taking a toll on the Mexican garrison. Even so, not all was lost for the defenders, as their position was solid. The battle continued to rage, until on the third day, the Mexican garrison ran out of powder and shot. De Ugartecha surrendered and was allowed to leave with a personal guard aboard a ship bound for Mexico.

The Mexican military commander at San Antonio de Bexar sent emergency orders for the nearest Mexican troops, stationed in Nacogdoches, to relieve the embattled garrison. The commander at Nacogdoches, Colonel Jose de la Piedras, a noted federalist and friend of General Santa Anna, arrived at Velasco after the fort had fallen.

On assessing the situation, he returned to Anahuac and relieved Bradford of his command and placed him under arrest. He restored order and civil rights in Liberty and Anahuac and released the prisoners. He then sent most of his men back to the Brazos to set about repairing the fort at Velasco. In his official report, he commended the militia for their actions in support of the best interests of Mexico.

In July, a regiment of four hundred Mexican soldiers, under the command of Colonel Jose Antonio Mexia, arrived at Brazosport. He informed Piedras and the colonists that Santa Anna had defeated Bustamonte. He further praised Piedras and the Texan militia for their apparent support of Santa Anna.

Further conflict with Mexico had been narrowly avoided by stumbling into the winning side of a civil war. Santa Anna's supporters were given the choice military appointments in Texas and other parts of Mexico. Bustamonte's supporters were exiled, jailed or executed. We breathed a collective sigh of relief for the peaceful respite we had been granted. But the dogs of war had been unleashed and their appetite for blood had not yet been satisfied.

Texans great and small heralded the assent of Santa Anna as the savior of Mexico. Things would now get better. I took my gold medallion of Santa Anna out and showed it again to Nancy and the family when we had gathered to celebrate his victory over Bustamonte. "General Santa Anna gave this to me for helping him obtain supplies to help him fight the rebels in Mexico a long time ago. He said he would never forget my service to him. I wonder if he would even remember my name?"

It was passed admiringly from person to person. It had lost little of its luster after so many years.

Lucius raised his glass of Nancy's homemade wine to toast the great man. "To General Santa Anna, may he live long and prosper. God bless Texas."

In August, the ayuntamiento, or town council, of San Felipe requested a state-wide convention to meet there on October 1, 1832. A representative was to be sent from each town or district. I would represent the Navasota District and Rob would represent the Upper Brazos District.

When the time finally arrived, I traveled with Rob on the *Brazos Belle* down river to San Felipe. The dear steamship would serve as our residence while we were attending the convention, as the accommodations in San Felipe were scarce and of poor quality.

In all, fifty-eight delegates were present. Those few towns beyond the Colorado, including San Antonio, declined to attend. After much talk and endless discussion, arguments and a few fist fights, the convention adopted a simple petition to be sent to the government of Tejas y Coahuila at Saltillo, with a copy to the national assembly in Mexico City.

We requested that tariffs be relaxed to encourage the growth and export of cotton and the importation of farm equipment. We asked that the ban on further immigration from the United States be repealed. Finally, we petitioned that Texas be separated from Coahuila to become an independent state within the Republic of Mexico.

Our petition had to be presented through the governmental chain of command. At its entry into the political process, Ramon Musquiz, political chief for Texas in San Antonio, ended its life and dashed our hopes. He declared that the convention had been an illegal assembly and annulled all actions taken by that body. Perhaps when Santa Anna became president, our hopes would be fulfilled. We did not know how wrong we were to place any hope for Texas in his bloody hands.

On an overcast late fall day, the fate and future of Texas was profoundly effected. There was no fanfare or ceremony. The only observers of this momentous arrival were a pair of white tail does. For on December 2, 1832, a rumpled giant of a man, mounted on an humble gray mule, splashed through an unnamed crossing of the Red River into Texas. He was dressed in greasy buckskins, heavily beaded in the Cherokee fashion. The Cherokee called him "Raven." To the rest of the world, he was known as Sam Houston. His unimpressive arrival in Texas would have unimagined consequences that would shape the fate of Texas for decades. The "Raven" had landed, and Texas would never be the same again.

12

Early 1833, Navasota Crossing, Austin's Colony, Texas

THE SKIES TO THE southwest held a massive line of gray clouds low on the horizon. As they drew closer, it could be seen that it was an army of anvil clouds sweeping diagonally toward the northeast. Thunder rumbled in the distance. As they gradually approached, the clouds took on an angry appearance as they grew in height and ferocity across the prairie to the west. Lightning could be seen inside the clouds, lancing to the ground as single and forked bolts.

Cody Teel's adopted son, Will, was near to hand, so I sent him to ring the bell in the church tower to alert everyone to the danger. "Will, you get over there fast and ring that bell until your arms fall off, then run to your daddy's cabin before the storm hits."

"You reckon it will be a bad storm?"

"I sure do. Now scat!"

The men and boys started filtering in from the fields riding harnessed mules. The wind had shifted to come from the southwest. It blew in ever increasing gusts. The scent of rain was heavy in the wind.

The lightning was crashing right along the river

now, the thunder coming simultaneously with the flash like the blast of a battery of cannon. The wind blew straight down off the front of the cloud bank, cold as ice. The sky was a sickening grayish-green as the rain began to blow in torrents.

Nancy and I closed and barred the shutters to protect the precious glass windows. Rain was pouring off the roof like a waterfall. Lightning popped all around us. Thunder shook the house to its foundations. Glassware rattled in the cupboard.

Hail began to fall. First, it was only pea to marble-sized, but then hail the size of eggs assaulted the tile roof. The pounding of the hail on the tile and the crashing of the thunder reminded me of the battle of New Orleans. The lightning came in blinding flashes that penetrated every corner of the cabin. The rain was blowing in horizontal sheets, parallel to the ground. The voice of the wind and the rain reached a howling pitch, interrupted by the deafening thunder.

The storm raged for a quarter of an hour, then left as quickly as it had started. When I stepped out on the porch, rainwater was standing in every direction.

A roaring sound came from the west that I did not recognize at first. Then I realized it was the Navasota. I slogged across the muddy ground, around hail piled high by wind and water, until I could see the river. It was running higher and faster than I had ever seen it. The ferry had been ripped from the landing and was nowhere in sight. The ground a hundred feet back from the river shook with the fury of the churning water.

I left the spectacle of the river behind and saddled a good steady horse to ride around to check on the neighbors. Many of the wood shingle roofs would need extensive repairs. The fruit trees had not yet broken bud that spring, but even so, they had been stripped of many of the smaller branches as had the trees along the river.

I rode north to check on the livestock. The mules and cattle were fine, but I had lost a nice young filly to the hail. The mare stood protectively over her lifeless foal. She turned and nuzzled it repeatedly. I used a rawhide rope and dragged the little horse out of the pasture and into the woods across the river road. The mare stood nickering over the rail fence to the baby that would never return.

As I rode back inside the fort I saw Nick standing outside his cabin. He pointed to the curled and beaten cypress shingles and gaps where they were missing entirely. "Guess Kassie is gonna have me fixin' that tomorrow."

The wheat and oats had been laid flat. But it had not yet begun to head, so it should recover somewhat. A few days of clear dry weather would see it standing up a little better.

The noxious smell of burnt hair and charred flesh led Cody to discover a cluster of three of his cattle that had been killed by lightning. He had found them still smoking, but too damaged to try to salvage. He left them for the buzzards and coyotes to clean up.

By the next day, the settlement was buzzing with debris being hauled away and new shingles being cut and nailed into place. A pair of bay mules strained as they turned the pole that powered the belts to our huge saw. Heavy planks were already being cut to build a new, larger ferry. We would have to wait for the river to go down before we could even consider floating the ferry.

Rob arrived in late March. He had tales to tell and news from Mexico. "I tell you, Aaron, that was one heck of a storm. It beat up our roof and hurt the winter grain some, but I guess it could have been worse. The Applewhite's tile roof didn't have a scratch."

"It was about the same here with the hail, crops and roof damage. I was glad we had a tile roof, too. Did you notice the new ferry? I figure the old one is somewhere in Galveston Bay by now."

"The new one is a dandy. It can carry twice the load. Who built it?"

"Joe Morgan and his son, Logan. Now, Rob, I know you well enough that you didn't ride forty miles to talk about the weather."

"No, I didn't. Word came to Brazosport that General Santa Anna was named president March 1. When the news got to San

Felipe, they called for a second convention to be held on April 1. I guess we'll be traveling together again."

San Felipe was humming with activity. The talk was that Santa Anna was just what this country needed. He would restore a federalist type government. There was renewed hope that Texas could become an individual state in the Republic of Mexico, no longer just an after thought, joined to the state of Coahuila.

Rob and I stayed aboard the *Belle*. When the second convention was called to order April 1, 1833, I met Sam Houston for the first time. He was a huge man with a big head, hands and feet, and a big mouth to match. He was dressed in beaded deer skins and moccasins. His long curly brown hair was pulled together and tied in the back. I couldn't decide if I liked him or not. He seemed to be an expert on every subject the convention addressed.

"Where the heck did that ol' bag of wind come from?" Rob asked.

"He's the representative from Nacogdoches, Sam Houston. He was a United States Senator from Tennessee and then Governor there, too. He's friends with Ol' Hickory."

"Well, if he's friends with Andy Jackson, I guess he can't be all bad."

The convention settled on the same requests as before. We asked for relaxed tariffs, a repeal on the ban of American immigration, and statehood within Mexico for Texas. This time, in anticipation of a favorable response, a provisional state constitution was drafted. Stephen Austin was going to hand carry our petition to Saltillo and Mexico City. We left in optimistic high spirits that Santa Anna would support us.

The summer of 1833 will forever be remembered as the summer that cholera came to Texas. Victims of cholera began with fever and chills. Soon, a terrible cramping diarrhea began that was characterized by white mucus in the stools. Many died of dehydration at that stage. Those who survived developed very cold hands, feet and legs, accompanied by horrible muscle aches and unstoppable vomiting. Some who survived the first stage died during the second. The very young and the very old died like flies. Healthy children and adults had a good chance of recovery if there was someone to care for them, as they were too sick to fend for themselves.

At Navasota Crossing, the cholera hit us hard. Little Francis got it first, then our older children. Finally, Nancy got it. I had caught cholera once in my travels to Mexico before I had married. It was my understanding that most folks who had it once and recovered usually did not get it again. Nancy helped care for the others until she was too ill. The older children at first were able to make it to the outhouse or use the slop jar, but soon were too weak to do even that. I emptied the chamber pots into a bucket and carried the filth away where I poured it in a hole in the ground far from our wells.

Francis died during the first stage of the illness from dehydration, I suppose. I buried her in the small cemetery in the meadow south of the settlement. I said a simple prayer for her as I laid her in the ground wrapped in a sheet. I wept and mourned her loss as I continued to care for the other children and Nancy. A few days later, our youngest boy, Joseph, died. I buried him beside his sister. With the others so gravely ill, I had no time to grieve, but I felt the loss of the two children in the pit of my stomach as a dull ache and heaviness that was with me every day.

I boiled oatmeal for Nancy and the children to eat. I gave them fresh water with a pinch of sugar and salt to drink. The rest of the day was consumed by bathing my patients and washing bed linens and clothes.

As Nancy got stronger, I helped her walk to the cemetery where we found thirteen other fresh graves. One in six persons living in Navasota Crossing had died. All but a few adults had been stricken. My family slowly regained their health, but our hearts were broken at the loss of our precious little ones. It was a summer we would never forget.

13

Spring 1834, Navasota Landing, Austin's Colony, Texas

SHIPS FLOWED INTO Galveston and Brazosport from all over the United States, the Caribbean and Mexico. There was regular passenger service from New Orleans, Vera Cruz and Tampico. With the passengers came news, and Captain Rob was there once a week. He was a link to the outside world, and the news he received was usually only days to weeks old.

In the spring of 1834, Tanner Lane again made a forced ride on a relay of horses from Louisiana Landing to Navasota Crossing to bring us news. "Colonel Turner, good to see you, sir. Captain Rob asked me to get this to you in person. It's mostly good news."

"Thanks, Tanner. Got any children yet?"

"Working on it, Reverend," he grinned.

"Nancy is still pretty weak, but Louisa will fix you something to eat and drink. Did the cholera hit y'all as hard as it hit here?"

"Yes, sir, it sure did. We lost a few folks and even some of the slaves. I thought I was gonna die."

"We lost Francis, the baby, and little Joseph. I guess

every one lost some one." I felt hot tears in the corners of my eyes.

"Take the upstairs bedroom on the southwest corner and get some rest."

He ate a prodigious amount of warmed up biscuits, ham and eggs, washed down with a whole pot of coffee. I guess after the kind of ride he had made, he deserved it. I noticed that Gray Jamison was handy, so I sent him to tend to all four of Tanner's horses.

I read Rob's letter out loud to Nancy and Louisa. "Stephen Austin wrote a letter to a friend expressing his hope that Texas might someday be annexed to the United States. It fell into the hands of the Mexican government at Saltillo. He was arrested for treason. He has been transferred to prison in Mexico City."

Nancy gasped, but Louisa did not seem to understand the gravity of the situation.

Santa Anna and the Mexican legislature passed a package of reforms. Anglo-American settlers could buy land directly from the government of Mexico at fair prices. Texas' representation in the legislature was increased from two to three members. Non-Mexican companies could do business in Texas.

"Daddy, I know we have been doing that for a long time. And didn't you buy some of our land from the Mexican government?"

"Louisa, when we came here, we swore oaths and became Mexican citizens. We can vote, hold office, buy and sell. I think this provision has to do with foreign owned companies doing business in Mexico. Now as for the land, I bought some directly from the government of Spain, darling, even before the Mexican government had set up shop."

"Nancy, look here. This provision makes English and Spanish both the official languages of Texas! They are allowing new settlement contracts; we are allowed to have trial by jury, not just a hearing before an alcalde. This is much more than I could have ever hoped to happen."

"Logan! Logan Morgan! Run to the church and ring the bell!"

As the crowd gathered in front of our house, I read the news from our porch. Every one was surprised and happy. This was an unexpected blessing for all of us; all but Stephen Austin. His tragedy was lost somewhere in our euphoria over the reforms Austin had worked so hard to achieve.

The roads were once again filled with settlers, most of whom were heading farther west, but some took up land near us. Others settled near Louisiana Landing and along the Camino Real between the two settlements. It was a time of prosperity, peace and hope for the future.

Our mill was busy for weeks making corn meal and for months ginning and baling cotton. We had been blessed with good rains and abundant crops.

When we made our annual trip to take our cotton to market, it was January before the ginning was finished. It took five rafts to get it all down river. On meeting Rob at Groce's plantation, we learned that Stephen Austin had been released from prison on bond, but he was still waiting in Mexico City for a hearing.

The spring of 1835 saw a surge of even more immigrants on the Camino Real. Our settlement prospered from the trade and services. Some of the settlers took up grants south of us along the river, and others claimed land across the Navasota. The ferry was busy from daylight until dark seven days a week. Logan Morgan, who was running the ferries, was one tired teenager. That gave him less time to get into trouble.

Nick became a father again with a son named Matthew. Cody, Chance, Lucius, and Marcus all had their first children. That meant that Nancy and I were grandparents.

The capital of Coahuila y Tejas was moved to Monclova, hundreds of miles closer to Texas. The national government seemed pro-immigrant and pro-Texan. Life was good. It had been said that nothing good lasts forever.

That spring would see a series of events that would hasten the inevitable clash of cultures that had been slowly approaching for generations. Santa Anna dissolved the National Congress and the state legislatures. He declared himself the dictator of Mexico. He pronounced himself the "Napoleon of the West." He seated a new congress of hand-picked supporters.

His apparent liberal federalist government had been a ruse to gain power. He was beginning to show his true colors. The laws we so recently celebrated were repealed.

The legislature at Monclova was ordered to dissolve and was to be replaced by a military government at Saltillo. Our friends at Monclova refused to disband. All states in Mexico were abolished and reorganized into military districts. Mexico was once again thrown into a violent civil war.

The Mexican states were shocked at their loss of statehood and democratic principles. They raised state militias in armed resistance to Santa Anna. One by one, the rebellious states were violently crushed.

The most vigorous resistance was encountered in Zacatecas. When it fell, Santa Anna allowed his troops to rape and pillage for two days before restoring order. Over two thousand civilians were brutally slain.

During this time of chaos, a well-placed bribe allowed Stephen Austin to leave Mexico City. He gradually started the long journey back to Texas. Once he reached Vera Cruz, he was able to secure passage to New Orleans, and finally, back to his beloved Texas. He landed in Brazoria, September 1, 1835 and he reached San Felipe soon after by steamer.

Things continued to deteriorate. The legislature of Coahuila y Tejas was attacked by the troops of Santa Anna's brother-in-law. They were defended by loyal federalist troops, but they were crushed by General Cos' much larger force. The legislators were arrested and imprisoned.

In Texas, William Travis organized a body of men who over-ran the small Mexican garrison at Anahuac and took control of the customs office. War had come to Texas.

14

September 1835, Upper Brazos District, Austin's Colony, Texas

WORD OF THESE EVENTS spread across Texas like wildfire. Information was mixed with misinformation, and none of us knew the full truth.

I had incorporated the new men and boys of our settlement and district into our militia. We now mustered over one hundred and twenty men at arms. Chance was my second-in-command. In that capacity, I had promoted him to the rank of major. It sounded strange to hear him called Major Chance, but I was proud of him. Of course, his given name was Louis bon Chance, Junior, but I had known him as just Chance all his life. I sent him to warn the outlying settlers and all the militia to be ready for an immediate call up of the volunteers.

I took Lucius, Marcus and Cody with me and headed hard and fast for Louisiana Landing. When we arrived, we were fortunate to find the *Brazos Belle* tied to the dock.

Captain Rob was in the pilot house of the steamer. He called down to us, "I've been expecting y'all. You got here just in time. I'm making a run down river to see for myself what is going on. Cody, I know you may want to see your in-laws, but this boat is pulling out. All of you leave your horses for the slaves to tend. Grab your rifles and jump aboard."

The wood-fired boilers already had a head of pressure up, so Rob backed her into the center of the river and let the current bring her bow around. She was blowing lots of smoke and moving faster than I had seen Rob push her. Once the cook wasn't needed to get the paddle wheeler moving, he brought us something to eat and drink. After a quick meal, I joined Rob in the pilot house.

"Rob, this mess with Mexico looks bad."

"Yep. I got to know how bad. You heard what Santa Anna had his soldiers do to those poor folks in Zacatecas? I don't aim to see that happen here."

"How many can you muster in your militia?"

"We got better than sixty men, boys, and slaves. All of them have rifles and are pretty good shots. We haven't had time to get the folks from that new Fort Parker worked into the militia yet, so they won't be sending anybody."

We were able to catch Stephen Austin in his office, working by lamp light. His nephew, Moses, was there. The boys and I were glad to see him. He was growing into a strapping young man.

"Colonel Turner, Captain Contois. I can guess why you have come. Things are deteriorating rapidly. Santa Anna has sent his brother-in-law, General Cos, with a full regiment of five hundred men to reinforce San Antonio. They sailed in troop transport ships and landed at Copano Bay along the coast. They are marching along the San Antonio River as we speak. I do not know for certain what Santa Anna's intentions might be, but his actions at Zacatecas and Monclova have me concerned. There will be an official consultation here in San Felipe on the third of November."

"Colonel Austin, them Mexicans are going to catch hell if they try to treat us like they did those poor folks."

"It is certainly a very serious situation. I hope we can resolve it with negotiations, but stronger methods may be necessary."

I smiled at Austin's diplomatic approach and phrasing. I knew him well enough not to underestimate the man. He was always in perfect control of his emotions and words. He could bury anger where no one could see it, but it glowed silently in the darkness within him. He was not given to intemperate actions. He gathered his facts and made a decision based on his mind and not his heart. But the thin polite man had a spine of tempered steel. It might bend, but it would not break. He was a good man to follow in dangerous times.

"Colonel Austin, Moses. Thank you for your time. We will ask Captain Rob to take us back up river. We have crops to gather and other preparations to make. You may be assured of our full support if and when the need arises."

"I'm with you, Aaron. I told the boys to keep the steam up in the boiler. Colonel Austin, we'll be seeing you soon."

The river was running pretty full due to recent rains making it easier to continue our journey at night, although Rob did reduce the speed somewhat. An unseen log could tear the bottom out of the steamer or wreck her paddle wheel.

On our return, I answered as many questions as I could to our neighbors. There were still more questions than answers. We set about our fall harvest with a strange sense of urgency and foreboding. How could things have changed so dramatically in such a short time?

One night after dinner and putting the little ones to bed, Nancy came to me on the front porch. "Aaron, we need to talk."

If any words clutch at the heart of a married man, guaranteed to get his attention, she had spoken them. She had my full, undivided attention.

"This war is none of your doing. You have done all you can to obey the law and keep the peace and help folks feel safe here. The people look up to you. They need you to lead them. I know that may take you away from here for a while, and will put you in harm's way again. I'm not afraid and I want you to go. This place is worth fighting for. The only thing I ask is, if you can, leave Lucius and Marcus here to guard the settlement. They are newly married. And if they're here, I'll feel safer."

I blinked back tears. Nancy was speaking from her heart. She asked so little for herself, I could not even think of refusing her request. "Nancy, I knew when I brought you here there would be certain dangers. I never dreamed there would be a war. I have never intended to be anywhere but by your side. I feel like I've got to go and do all I can or we could lose everything."

We held each other tightly that fall night on the upstairs gallery of our fine home. We were worried and frightened, but knew the day was coming soon when action in defense of our home would be required.

Over in DeWitt's Colony, west of the Colorado and east of San Antonio a single four pounder cannon had been sent to help the settlement of Gonzales defend itself from frequent Comanche raids. Colonel Ugartecha, formerly the commander at Velasco, had given orders from San Antonio to retrieve the cannon.

First, he had sent a Lieutenant with a small escort to request its surrender. The citizens of Gonzales had made a flag with the words "Come and get it!" arching over the likeness of a small cannon. The young officer saw that retrieving the cannon was hopeless. He rode back to report to his commanding officer.

Colonel Ugartecha had plenty of experience with these Texans, all of it bad. He reluctantly sent Captain Castaneda with a troop of lancers to retrieve the cannon.

When Captain Castaneda arrived, he found a breastwork of logs along the opposite river bank with the cannon protecting the ford and dozens of angry, well-armed Texans sheltered behind the hastily built defenses.

Captain Castaneda sent a young lieutenant across the ford, under the protection of a white flag, to explain that they were under orders to retrieve the cannon. His horse received a hard smack on the rump which sent the horse and rider at a gallop back across the river. No one seems sure who fired the first shot, but a general fight erupted.

The Mexican cavalry tried to force the crossing, but the determined fire of rifles from a protected position proved too much for the Mexican lancers. The cannon had been loaded with an unusually large amount of gunpowder, old chain, horseshoes and nails. When it fired into the packed Mexican cavalry, it created havoc in their troop.

Castaneda wisely realized that his troop of lancers could not displace entrenched riflemen supported by a cannon without suffering tremendous casualties. With a salute of his saber to the Texans, he gathered his men to leave.

A small body of Texans foolishly mounted a pursuit, but found themselves in extreme danger from the lancers. Only their rapid retreat across the river to the safety of the barricade and cannon saved them. The Battle of Gonzales, such as it was, went down as a win on the Texan side of ledger.

Militias from all across Texas mobilized. Volunteers began to arrive from outside of Texas, too. There was a constant stream of men from Tennessee, Louisiana, Arkansas, and as far away as Alabama, heading west on the Camino Real.

These were not settlers traveling with families. They were men who had come for a fight. They came on foot, riding horses or mules carrying provisions, rifles and powder.

They didn't seem to know exactly why they had come. Word had spread in the United States of Santa Anna's brutal dictatorship. With his attention now focused on "Americans" living in Texas, these frontiersmen came to fight. Was it to fight for Texas' freedom? I rather doubted that. Perhaps it was more of a combination of the long-held American hatred of dictators, and a dislike for "foreigners" abusing Americans where ever they lived. What ever the reason, they came to fight, and we welcomed them in our struggle.

The life-line to the United States was only one hundred yards from our front porch in the form of the Camino Real. We provided camp grounds for these volunteers south of the settlement in the pasture there. We replenished their stores of food as best we could from our store houses and corn cribs.

They were farmers, clerks, lawyers and loggers. Some referred to themselves as "filibusters," a term which loosely translated into unpaid mercenaries. From my dealings with the Fredonian Rebellion, filibusters meant trouble makers looking for a fight. But Texas needed these men, whether patriots or rabble. If there had been a last thread of hope of restoring peace with Mexico, it was now broken.

I sent Chance with gifts to our allies, the Wichita to the northwest and the nearer Tonkawa just to our north, to ask their help by warning us of any Comanche or Mexican raids headed our direction. With our current preoccupation with the Mexicans to the southwest, it would be a disastrous time for them to strike.

We received word of the "Consultation" to convene at San Felipe on the third of November. Rob and I would again represent our respective districts.

Austin exercised his authority as commanding officer of all the militias in his colony. Indeed, he was our own commander. But the militias from other colonies, and the out of state volunteers, proved an independent lot. They elected their own officers who only reluctantly agreed to follow Austin as long he was leading the direction they wanted to go.

General Cos arrived in San Antonio de Bexar with his five hundred men, bringing the total to six hundred and fifty men. He had been sent to fortify the city, as San Antonio was a vital link in the over-land link with Mexico City and the army led by Santa Anna.

He built gun emplacements for the twelve cannon that straining oxen had laboriously hauled up the banks of the San Antonio River. Included in the armament was a massive eighteen pounder. He mounted it atop the ruined chapel of an abandoned mission called the Alamo. He sent mounted patrols out to screen for the approach of any Texan forces, and to gather into San Antonio any odds and ends of Mexican soldiers from various minor posts.

A body of militia set out from Matagorda to seize the lightly defended outpost, Presidio la Bahia, on the banks of the San Antonio River at Goliad. They were able to muster one hundred and twenty five men.

The Mexican garrison, under Colonel Sandoval, consisted of only fifty men. Many of them were not prime troops, but those more typically assigned to garrison duty. On the morning of October 10, 1835, a former slave made a savage attack with an axe against the wooden postern gate of the fort under the cover of his comrades' rifles. The door gave way, and the Texans flooded into the fort. With enemies now on both sides of the walls, the Mexican position was indefensible. The outnumbered Mexicans surrendered.

The Texans grandly renamed the old presidio "Fort Defiance." Defiant it was; fortress perhaps, but wise it was not. The Texans had no means to support fixed defensive positions with a much larger professional army headed their way. This stood as a roadblock on the main resupply route from the Gulf of Mexico to San Antonio. General Cos was now in a difficult position. His primary supply route to the sea had been vulnerable at best, but now it was severed. At San Antonio the Mexican army dug in and waited.

15

Fall 1835, Navasota Crossing, Austin's Colony, Texas

WORD REACHED US that on October 12, Stephen Austin had declared that Texas was in a state of war with Mexico. The following day, he assumed the role of Commander and Chief of "The People's Army." He had set out for San Antonio with four hundred fifty three men and two six pounder cannon. He had sent orders for all available militias to reinforce him at San Antonio.

Nancy and I talked far into the crisp fall night, huddled together under a quilt on the upstairs gallery. "Aaron, I'll be alright here. Lucius and Marcus aren't happy about staying behind, but they understand. They are going to move back into the house here with their wives and little ones. There aren't any Mexican soldiers anywhere near here and the Comanche are far away."

"They may not stay far away."

"It would take a mighty big bunch of Indians to attack a fort this size with a handful of able bodied men on the walls and every woman and child in the place able to load and shoot like a man. I've fought Comanche before, and I could do it again."

"Yes, and I was right here next to you, and once they darn near got in the gate."

"We fixed the problem with the gate. They would have half a dozen shotguns loaded with buckshot pouring both barrels to them if they attack the gate now. The older kids can handle themselves, and there will be some men here. Aaron, you can't be two places and they need you and your militia at San Antonio."

"All right. Rob and I have got to go to San Felipe, and Chance will be following with the rest of the militia. Did you know I made him a major? Seems not too long ago he was just sixteen. I'm going to leave twenty steady men here to keep you women from getting all the glory. I'm going to order all the outlying settlers to move into the fort. Do you ever wish I had never brought you here?"

"I certainly do not! I love it here. We have been blessed beyond our wildest dreams."

We held each other there on the gallery all night long until the purple light of dawn told me it was time to go. I kissed the children and Nancy.

Chance, Lucius and Marcus were given their last minute orders. Lucius was now a lieutenant in the militia. He would be in charge once Chance rode out. I traveled half way to the Brazos the first night and reached Louisiana Landing by early the next afternoon. The air was thick with tension. Their settlers had also moved in nearer the stockade and the Applewhite's formidable house. The militia was getting organized.

Rob found me. "Well, Colonel Turner, we are sure in the stew now."

"How close to being ready are you with your militia now?"

"You already saw that we are moving everybody in closer. I made Applewhite a lieutenant of militia and am going to leave him here with his twelve black men and all the women and boys who can shoot. I think they'll be safe enough. The militia is supposed to cross the river on the ferries and hot foot it down to San Felipe as soon as the corn is in the cribs. The slaves can start picking cotton with a rifle on their backs. We'll help finish up with the cotton when we get back from whatever we are going to be doing."

We set out on the *Brazos Belle* the next morning and arrived in San Felipe before dark. There was already militia gathering there. When they tried to convene the Consultation, there weren't enough delegates for a quorum. Many of them had pushed on to San Antonio. They sent Sam Houston to retrieve the voting delegates so we could get on with business. When he returned with the stragglers, a quorum was present, so the meeting was called to order. There was an urgent need for our proceedings to be as legally correct as possible if we had a chance for recognition from the United States and other countries.

Sam Houston asked to address the assembly.

"Looks like the "Ol' Raven" is gonna start squawking again," Rob grumbled.

"Men, here is the situation in San Antonio so far. Austin began there in charge of four hundred and twenty-three militia and two six pounder cannon. He sent Ben Milam's mounted company out to scout. They skirmished with a handful of Mexican soldiers. Austin has moved his camp from Cibolo Creek to Salado Creek, just about five miles from the outskirts of San Antonio. Our Tejano friend and ally, Juan Seguin, brought a troop of thirty- seven mounted vaqueros to join Austin. Another company of seventy-six Anglo militia came up from Victoria."

"Jim Bowie and James Fannin led a reconnaissance-in-force which captured one of the forward Mexican outposts at Mission Espada. They managed to capture Mission Concepcion, just two miles from San Antonio. The Mexicans launched a counterattack, but got their tails whipped. Austin has got his camp there now with about six hundred men."

"General Cos has been scraping together reinforcements from every small garrison from San Antonio to the Nueces. He appears to be commanding better than a thousand mixed troops of lancers, infantry, engineers and artillery. He has twenty cannon mounted at strategic places, including one danged huge eighteen pounder mounted on the old Alamo mission."

Henry Smith was chairman of the Consultation. He also happened to be one of the most disagreeable men I had ever met. "Well, Houston, if you are through flapping your jaws, I got a question for you. Can we take 'em?"

Houston flushed with anger, but held his temper. "With additional reinforcements, I think it can be done. So your answer, to make it simple for you, is yes."

The assembled group elected a slate of provisional government officers. Henry Smith was to be president. Sam Houston was appointed Commander-in-Chief of all the Texan forces not currently under Austin's control. Austin and two others were appointed envoys to the United States, specifically to seek financial assistance for Texas.

Houston ordered all available militias to converge on San Antonio. Rob and I had plenty of work to do. We quickly steamed up river to Louisiana Landing. I rode on to Navasota Crossing using a relay of horses, making it in a hard six hours. Such a ride was getting to be pretty tough for me, as I was fifty-two. This war was going to be hard on all of us.

The militia quickly assembled. I detailed a company of twenty trusted men to guard the settlement and the crossing. I had appointed Lucius as the Lieutenant in charge, and made Marcus his sergeant. That left one hundred of us to ride back to the Brazos, join up with Rob's company, and head to the siege of San Antonio. Chance remained regimental major, while Nick and Cody Teel, Richard Moore and Joe Morgan were all lieutenants. Red Wolf, in response to a previous request, sent five of his Tonkawa braves as scouts. I was mighty glad to have them, as nothing escaped their attention.

Every man carried his best rifle, a couple of pistols, extra flints, powder and shot, with a tomahawk or fighting knife tucked in his belt. They carried morrals filled with jerky, parched corn, corn meal and salt, and a little coffee if they had it. Each took a jacket of some type, a bedroll, and extra clothes and a canteen. Most of the men filled another couple of morrals with oats for their horse. We took a dozen pack mules with cooking gear and extra supplies.

Tanner Moore, Gray Jamison and Logan Morgan were all about sixteen. They could handle themselves and we needed them with us. I just hoped to bring them home alive.

I had clutched Nancy and the children tightly to me before riding west on the Camino Real. When I had fought at New Orleans, I was a bachelor with no one waiting for me or depending on me. Leaving for war with a wife and children at home was a new experience for me, one I did not like. I had shaken hands with both Marcus and Lucius. "You both know I have loved you as if you were my own flesh and blood. Please be careful and take care of your mother and the little ones."

"We will, Papa Aaron," Marcus said. He hadn't called me that in a long time.

"We will Colonel Turner," Lucius said. The burden on his shoulders was evident in his voice. "We're counting on you getting back, too."

When the regiment had gathered, we forded the river, as the Navasota was low. It would be a long difficult road before us.

We camped that night along the Camino Real where we had seen the wolves pull down the old buck. I wondered, in the saga unfolding before us, if we would suffer the fate of the prey or the predators.

We arrived on the banks of the Brazos the next day. Rob's sixty member militia company was assembled. Forty of them would ride with us and twenty would remain behind to secure the ferry and protect the settlement. Settlers from across the area had gathered at Rob's small stockade and the Applewhite's house for safety. William Applewhite had been appointed lieutenant of militia and would be in charge at Louisiana Landing. Rob said he believed Applewhite would have been happier to have been made a general.

At daylight the next morning, we crossed the Brazos in groups on the twin ferries. The first contingent across set up in skirmish formation a hundred yards out from the bank in case there were Mexican patrols on the loose. All one hundred and forty of us, plus our five Tonkawa scouts were finally across. We remounted and closed up in road formation as we headed southwest down the Camino Real. The scouts disappeared into the brush ahead and to both sides of our column. We rode with loaded rifles across the pommels of our saddles. There was a sense that our future depended on our actions; our lives and futures hung in the balance.

16

November 1835, San Antonio de Bexar, Texas

THE NOVEMBER weather was dry and clear as we pushed steadily toward San Antonio. I had not been there since our exploratory trip in 1817, and I was not anxious to return. Once we had crossed the Colorado River, we had been in the danger zone. Our scouts had found no signs of Mexican patrols anywhere, nor had they seen any evidence of Comanche in the area.

Our column of one hundred and forty armed men would be relatively safe from Comanche war bands. However, if we met with Mexican lancers of similar strength, we would be in trouble. We had little defense against the wicked long lances. Once we had fired our rifles and pistols, we could be cut to pieces by the surviving lancers.

"Gray, ride back and ask Captain Contois to join me at the front of the column."

"Captain Contois, sir?"

"Our old friend Captain Rob, if you please. Oh, get Major Chance, too."

"Yes sir, Colonel."

He touched the spurs to his handsome young horse and galloped down the line. He soon returned with Rob and Chance.

"Rob, Chance, I've been studying on a problem and want to see what you think. If we are met with Mexican lancers, we have to be prepared. If most of us are holding empty guns, we are going to be in a world of hurt. Tell each squadron to have the men count off in even and odd numbers. Each sergeant is to have only half of his men fire at a time if we come under attack. The other half should hold their fire as long as possible while the others reload. If a body of lancers tries to flank us, the squadron at the end of the column should wheel to meet the threat in two ranks. They were to alternate their fire, also.

"Aaron, I think that might work. What if they get behind us?" Chance asked.

"Half of each company will wheel to face them. Then they are to alternate fire. And if that happens, God help us all."

We finally reached the hacienda of my old friend, Don Fernando de Zavala. I rode ahead with an escort of twenty men to see what type of reception we would receive. It had been eighteen years since I had seen Don Fernando. I did not know if he even still lived. More importantly, I did not know his politics.

As we approached the large adobe house and attached adobe corrals, I saw that heavily armed vaqueros were stationed around the firing ports along the roof and the corral. Gun barrels appeared from every gun loop of the lower walls. An armed group of ten mounted men challenged us as we approached the hacienda under the protective cover of the guns along the walls.

One of the vaqueros spoke. "Would you please identify yourself?"

"I am Lieutenant Colonel Aaron Turner of the Texas militia. I command a regiment riding to join the siege at Bexar. I am an old friend of Don Fernando, although I have not seen him in many years. Is he well?"

"Yes, Colonel. He is very well for a man of his age. I will ask him if you are welcome."

Before the vaquero was able to turn his horse, the front door of the hacienda was thrown open. A distinguished white haired hidalgo walked in erect confidence directly to us. I recognized him as Don Fernando.

"I had to see with my own eyes that it is you, my friend. I give you the hospitality of my hacienda. Welcome, Aaron!"

I immediately dismounted my horse and offered my hand. "It is good to see you are still strong and healthy. I have remembered your friendship and hospitality many times."

"Lieutenant Colonel, is it now? I remember you well! I have heard of your successful settlement on the Navasota River. Someone is always passing along the Camino Real with news. You and all your men are welcome. Do you ride to support Stephen Austin, that fool Ugartecha, or the even more foolish General Cos?"

"Stephen Austin."

"Then you are doubly welcome. Although I am a Mexican, I am weary of dictators. Santa Anna has crushed freedom in other parts of Mexico and will try to do so here. If you ride for freedom from tyranny, then you have my blessing."

"Thank you. We will have to leave in the morning."

"Yes, I had suspected that. But tonight we will feast." I showed my surprise. It was obvious I did not understand. "Aaron, a regiment raises a great deal of dust on the road. My vaqueros have watched you since you crossed the Rio Colorado. I have had young cattle killed and slowly roasting since last night to feed your men. Please allow my foreman to show you to your accommodations."

The same vaquero who had first spoken to us approached with an air of confidence. "Colonel Turner, we have made the corral ready for your horses and mules. There is cool water, fresh hay, oats and corn waiting for them. The patron has made rooms available for you and your officers in the house, and for your men in the large barns near the corrals. Wooden tubs, hot water, soap and towels have been made available for those who wish to bathe. The serving of the food will begin at sundown."

The horses were led into the protective walls of the adobe corrals and unsaddled. Their saddles, as well as the men's gear, were placed in the adobe and tile barns. Many took advantage of the opportunity to clean up before the feast.

I found a hot bath drawn for me in my room along with fresh clothes. A servant discretely took my road worn clothes to wash, repair and return them. A barber quietly knocked at my door to provide a haircut and shave. I felt like a new man.

Rows of benches and tables had been set up in the huge courtyard. Serving tables groaned under the huge mounds of beef cooked to tender perfection, along with beans and corn tortillas. I noticed no alcohol had been provided. Here, a man had to keep a clear head, and drunken friends could be as dangerous as sober enemies.

I listened while our young men talked of the fighting to come.

"I'll bet them Mexicans will turn tail and run when they see us Texas boys mean business." Logan bragged. He, Tanner, and Gray were full of vinegar.

"We fought Comanche and whipped 'em. These Mexicans can't be near as bad as them," Gray added.

"Dad showed me some of their muskets. They're smooth bore, mostly .69 caliber, and some even bigger. He said they can't hit a log barn at more than seventy-five yards." Tanner's father, Richard Moore, was the settlement's blacksmith and gunsmith.

I felt the need to join the conversation. "Boys, they got a lot of guns just like you said. But they have rifle companies with guns every bit as good as yours. And those big ol' guns can hurt a man pretty bad up close, especially when they have a bayonet on the end of them. The Mexicans have got some cavalry that can hold their own with any Comanche. Stick together. Always keep one gun loaded. Keep under cover when you can. This isn't going to be a picnic on the river."

The morning of November 16 we found Austin's camp. Such a large reinforcement was obviously welcome, swelling the Texan force to over six hundred men. General Cos now commanded more than twelve hundred men.

Our Tonkawa scouts had served their purpose and left without even spending the night. We made camp on the grounds of the old Mission Concepcion. My men were fresh and ready to fight. Some of those volunteers who had been there longer were ready to go home.

Once Austin learned of his new role as emissary to the United States, he transferred command to Colonel Edward Burleson. Austin made his way with all haste to the coast to set sail for the United States. We were to later learn that he made impassioned speeches from New Orleans to Washington that stirred support in men, money and materials for the Texas cause.

On November 18, 1835, the *New Orleans Grays* marched sharply into our camp. The volunteers were dressed in fine gray uniforms and the best clothes a man could buy. They carried the finest rifles and marched in step to a snappy drummer. Their military precision and disciplined behavior were relatively foreign to the Texas militia. They were a sight to behold and an encouraging reinforcement.

Erastus "Deaf" Smith was an important member of the Texas militia. He was a full time scout and one of the finest trackers in Texas. He had earned his name from the fact that he was very hard of hearing, but not completely deaf. Soon after the arrival of the *New Orleans Grays,* he reported finding a large pack train of horses and mules escorted by about fifty to a hundred Mexican soldiers. Colonel Burleson sent Jim Bowie with a hand-picked platoon of expert riflemen to be accompanied by a larger mounted troop. Our regiment, the Northeast District Regiment, was chosen for the job, as we were well mounted on fresh horses, well armed and rested.

I addressed our regiment. "Men, we have our first assignment fighting Mexican soldiers. There is a pack train with a heavy guard supporting it. Our job is to drive off the guard and capture the supply train. Rob, I'm sorry, but they need your company to stay here to continue the siege."

Blake Lane, who was a sergeant with the Upper Brazos Company attached to our regiment, spoke up. "Colonel Turner, we been hearin' all kind of rumors that pack train is carrying the Mexican payroll in silver. We sure want to get in on that."

"Blake, I never knew you to get too far away where there was a dollar to be had." The rest of the assembled men laughed at the truth of that statement. "Any goods or valuables will be turned over to Colonel Burleson to support the welfare of the whole army. I doubt any of you came here expecting to get rich."

We set out on November 26 and caught the Mexicans crossing a dry ravine about a mile outside of San Antonio. The marksmen opened fire, aiming for the officers. There was a brief sharp fight. The Mexicans broke off and headed for the safety of San Antonio, leaving the pack train behind.

We gathered up the horses and mules and began to search the panniers. To our great surprise and disappointment, they contained hay for the cavalry mounts trapped inside San Antonio, a little salt, a few sacks of oats, and dried beans. Well, at least our horses would be eating well. The "battle" known as "The Grass Fight" didn't amount to much, but we had been victorious, such as it was.

As winter settled in, supplies ran low and the morale of some of the men started to sag. After disagreement among the commanding officers, Jim Bowie left, taking his regiment with him back to San Felipe for rest and resupply. Counting our regiment, there were a little over four hundred men left to support the siege.

There was a very real concern that once General Cos realized how few our number, he would attack. He had enough men to easily overrun us. A sense of futility started to filter into our ranks, as more companies discussed going home. Our regiment would remain on duty as long as needed. However, we had come a long way, leaving our families vulnerable, to run the Mexican army out of San Antonio and all the way across the border. Would we just give up, after doing so little, and go home?

Ben Milam, one of the oldest combatants in the camp, and one of the most respected, stood in the back of a wagon to speak to the discouraged volunteers. He argued with passion that we ought to attack while we still had the men and the means. "Who will follow Old Ben Milam?"

His speech had so inflamed our passions that all one hundred and forty men in my command, plus another hundred and fifty from another regiment agreed to do just that. I believe that we would have charged hell with half a bucket of water for Ben Milam.

In the pre-dawn darkness of December 5, we quietly assembled for the planned two-pronged attack. Rob approached me. "Reverend Turner, the men would appreciate it if you would lead us in prayer."

I agreed as the men crowded closely so that they could hear. Some knelt, others stood, but all uncovered their heads. "Merciful Father, we ask your blessing on us today. Guide and guard our footsteps. We ask, if it is Your will, that You will protect us and place victory within our hands. Have mercy on our souls and those of our enemies. Watch over our families in our absence. In Jesus name, Amen."

The men echoed "Amen."

There was no bugle or fanfare to announce our assault. Two adobe houses were chosen for their height as places to seize and hold. I led our regiment to attack the closest.

Nick, Chance and Cody bit into the adobe walls with picks as other men provided cover for them and protected our flanks from a counter-attack. A door sized hole was soon opened in the adobe wall and our men poured through the gaping hole. The inhabitants had fled, and there were no Mexican soldiers to oppose us.

We quickly sent men to the second story roof, as well as stationing them in ample numbers at each door and window. From this foothold, more men poured into the streets to expand our attack.

They were met with determined resistance from a platoon of Mexican soldiers. They blew trumpets to sound the alarm. Many more troops arrived and drove us back into the house. The men we had on the roof and second story windows kept them at bay.

A Mexican lieutenant led a platoon of about twenty men to attack the front door as other Mexicans poured a heavy fire to protect their approach. They reached the heavily barred oak door, but were not able to batter it down.

A stout Mexican sergeant left and returned with a heavy axe. Our men were not able to fire at the men huddled at the door, but worked misery and death on the covering soldiers in the street. Soon, the protective group of soldiers was forced to withdraw. The assaulting platoon was now without support, but still safe from our rifle fire.

I sent Chance and twenty men out the hole in the back wall of the adobe to work their way around the corner of the house. He intended to drive the Mexican soldiers away from the door.

Chance barked his orders so he could be heard over the skirmishing out front. "When we are around the corner, form two ranks. The front rank is to kneel. Fire on my orders."

As they wheeled around the corner and took their positions, the Mexicans were too preoccupied with their assault to notice them. A voice from across the street shouted a warning to them. As they turned to face the threat, Chance's men were ready.

"Front rank, fire!"

"Reload. Rear rank, fire!"

The twenty aimed shots at such close range had taken twelve lives and wounded two more. The remaining six men and the lieutenant turned to flee, as Mexican reinforcements appeared from their hiding places.

Bullets whizzed around the Texans as Chance ordered them back into the house. "Colonel Turner, we are bottled up in here where we can't fight or bring our guns to bear. We need to get men into the houses on either side of us."

"Chance, take the house to the right. Nick, you take the house on the left. I'll send men to reinforce you once you have it secure."

Once again the picks rang out on the crumbling adobe. As they broke through the walls, they encountered a few Mexican troops who fired as they retreated.

We reinforced both houses, and placed men on their roofs as before. Fortunately, there were no houses within rifle range taller than these three, so no one would be able to get above us. We chopped holes in the adobe walls to create more firing ports to cover the vulnerable doors.

Texan reinforcements now poured out of all three houses. The Mexican soldiers defending the houses across the street fought bravely.

Logan, Tanner, and Gray were in Nick's platoon. They had shot Indians from a distance, but desperate hand-to-hand fighting was new to them. They learned the value of the fast-handling tomahawks in close quarters.

Tanner and Logan used their muskets to parry the deadly fierce attack of a Mexican soldier armed with a musket and bayonet. Gray used his quickness for one wicked blow to the soldier's head with his tomahawk, killing him instantly.

Before they had time to think, other Mexicans took their places. Tanner used one of his huge saddle pistols at point blank range to kill a Mexican soldier whose bayonet had become entangled in his coat.

Logan had stepped back to reload as two Mexicans set upon Gray. Gray used his still loaded musket to deflect their bayonets. He knew he would be dead as soon as he fired it, as the surviving soldier would surely kill him. Logan came to his aid. He slammed the heavy rifle barrel into the head of the closest soldier, then shot the second soldier. As the first tried to rise, Gray clubbed him in the face with the butt of his rifle.

As more soldiers attacked them, they were able to use their tomahawks to grab the heavy muskets and jerk them aside. Once the bayonet was out of harm's way, the flashing blade of a heavy fighting knife in their left hands plunged into their enemies. Chance had taught them the art of killing well.

The sweat poured, streaking lines amid the powder stains and splattered blood on their faces as they waded side-by-side into the battle. They were rarely out of the sight of Joe Morgan or Richard Moore who were amazed at their sons.

Similar encounters occurred from house to house. The Mexicans fought fiercely, but slowly yielded street by street. The boys were exhausted. Their faces were blackened from powder smoke, their clothes stained with blood and gore of other men. Their youthful innocence had been lost at San Antonio. They were now hardened men of the frontier.

We were able to repulse numerous counter-attacks. Other Texan troops now controlled a large part of the city.

By December 7, we still held our position and other reinforcements had established another foothold from a different direction. We had the defenders in a pincher movement. Attacks issued from both points drove the Mexicans back further into San Antonio.

We had made significant gains, but lost Ben Milam to a musket ball. The boys saw first hand what a .75 caliber escopeta could do at close range, as it opened a hole in Milam's chest the size of a man's fist.

The other prong of the attack had met with similar success. We were able to consolidate the two positions, holding a large crescent of the crumbling adobe city.

General Cos fell back to the Alamo with about six hundred men as more and more Texans swarmed into the city. The Texan six pounders had been man-handled into the city where they hammered away at the old mission.

Most of the Mexican cannon had been placed around the perimeter of the besieged city and were out of position to threaten us. Some of the Mexicans' own cannon had been turned to fire into the Alamo and the plaza. The huge eighteen pounder cannon had been positioned with a field of fire directed outside the city. It was nearly impossible to decrease the elevation of the gun to direct fire at an enemy at the gates.

The Mexican troops outside the Alamo continued to mount stiff resistance in house to house fighting, selling their lives dearly. The Mexican troops had been trained to fight in traditional formations using classical European tactics. The hard-bitten Texans knew little of maneuver and European tactics, but they had cut their teeth on hand-to-hand combat.

By December 9, Cos ordered the remainder of his troops to pull back to support the Alamo. He left a company of fifty men and two light cannon to cover the retreat from the plaza into the Alamo.

His cavalry officers refused to be trapped within the walls of the old mission. Against direct orders, they took their one hundred and seventy-five men and managed to fight their way out of the embattled city. Disengaging from the Texan soldiers, they headed south at a gallop.

With this loss, and the relentless approach of the determined Texans, General Cos raised a flag of truce. There was no reinforcement expected. The Mexicans were now out-gunned by a force of almost equal size. It would be only a number of day or hours before the Texans would swarm into the old mission. General Cos could lead a counter-attack into the Texan cannons, with little hope of success. After hours of negotiations, the Mexicans surrendered on December 10. They pledged to leave Texas, never to return under arms.

Their departure left not a single Mexican garrison in Texas. But that was soon to change. The hounds of hell had been unleashed and their thirst for blood would not easily be quenched.

17

January 1836, Navasota Crossing, Austin's Colony, Texas

WE DID NOT TARRY long in San Antonio to savor our victory. We had no illusions that the war was over. The worst was yet to come. We spent one night as the guests of Don Fernando, but left early the next morning as we were anxious about our families. The good meal he provided for us, and the hay and grain for our horses, refreshed us all. He sent morrals of corn and oats for the livestock.

We pushed ourselves and our horses until we had the Colorado River behind us. Once we crossed those shallow waters, we felt we were heading home. We stopped only long enough to feed and water the horses. We would eat a cold midday meal and only cook up hot grub at night.

The wide, muddy Brazos finally spread out before us. We rang the bell to call the ferry, but the Louisiana Landing sentries had already seen us and started them across. Soon both ferries were carrying men and animals back into what we considered home country. Our rear guard was safely over before too long.

The folks at Louisiana Landing quickly began

preparing a big meal for all of us after they had greeted their loved ones. We chose to spend the night there. We had pushed hard for a long time. The next morning, we left early to make the hard forty miles that would take us home. We rested at the midway point, eating a cold lunch.

I once again saw the place where the wolves had killed the buck. Our struggle had begun, but was far from over. The first blood had been shed, but not the last. Once we reached the Navasota, we found the water low enough to ford. When I pushed my horse into those familiar waters, I felt the tension in my shoulders start to relax. I was home.

Lucius met me at the stockade gate. "Welcome home, Father. Things have been quiet here. I sure am glad to see you home. Did everyone else come back?"

"Hello, son. I'm glad to be back, too. We had only a few minor injuries. Tanner Lane caught a careless Texan bayonet in the rump, but it's a long way from his heart. Logan got creased by a musket ball on the right cheek, but it is healing to make a nice little scar. He seems right proud of it. Everyone made it home."

"What's the news of the war?"

"Son, those Mexicans fought like demons, but we have driven the Mexicans out of San Antonio and back across the border. But make no mistake, they will be back."

I saw Nancy in the distance, standing in the small cemetery across the road. I left my horse with Lucius and walked to join her.

Looking up, Nancy saw me and ran to embrace me. "Aaron, I am so glad you are back safely."

I held her as she quietly sobbed. "I thought I had lost you this time. I have been so lonely and worried while you were gone that I have been visiting Francis' and Joseph's graves every day. It just seems to help." I held her hand and walked with her to our home.

We sent our reports down river to San Felipe. We soon received news there was to be a third Convention March 2. This time the meeting was to be held at Washington-on-the Brazos, as San Felipe was deemed to be more at risk of a Mexican raid.

General Houston had sent orders to demilitarize San Antonio. The guns were to be removed and sent east. The Alamo compound and its guns that could not be moved were to also be destroyed. The remaining garrison was to evacuate east as soon as their demolition work was done and to join Houston's army at Gonzales.

His orders were ignored and the old mission was restored to fighting shape and reinforced. Many of the cannon were installed in bastions at the newly fortified Alamo, including the massive eighteen pounder. The walls Houston had ordered to be torn down were instead reinforced. The men who were to evacuate, instead chose to stay. They were determined to hold what they had won. The price for their bravery would be far greater than anyone could foresee.

In February 1836, a powerful cold front swept down from the north. It howled all the way to the coast. It pushed across the Nueces and the Rio Grande deep into northern Mexico.

Temperatures plunged; sleet and snow mixed with rain fell as far south as Saltillo, Tamaulipas and Chihuahua. General Santa Anna, President of Mexico, a dictator with the blood of vengeance in his eyes, drove his army of several thousand men relentlessly up the long overland road that stretched from Mexico City to San Antonio. General Urrea led a smaller army up the road that followed the coast from Tampico to Texas.

Santa Anna's supply train had proven inadequate. His quartermaster had failed to secure adequate wagons, horses, mules and carts. Even worse, there was not enough fodder for the animals, food for the men, and improper clothing and gear for winter campaigning.

Santa Anna commandeered every wagon, rickety cart, horse, mule or ox along the way. He found his men were completely unprepared for winter operations. They had few tents. They had only summer weight uniforms. Even worse, his soldiers had discarded their lightweight coats in the warmth of the early days of the march north.

When the cold front slammed into the Mexican army, they did not know that it would be one of the coldest ever seen in that part of Mexico. His army was unprepared. Men froze to death where they slept. Pack mules were found frozen to death where they stood, often with their packs still in place.

But Santa Anna drove them mercilessly northward. His pride had been insulted by those upstart Texans. His family honor had been smeared by his brother-in-law's surrender to the rag-tag Texan militia. He pushed his army forward to exact his revenge.

What the world had seen at Zacatecas would be nothing compared to what they would see in Texas. The self-proclaimed "Napoleon of the West" would impose his will on the rebellious Texans. This undisciplined rabble would feel the steel of his sword. On February 16, Santa Anna crossed the Rio Grande. Texas would soon feel his wrath, for the lion was among the lambs.

Word of Santa Anna's entry into Texas at the head of a huge army flashed across the Texan settlements like a bolt of lightning. I summoned an officers' call for our militia at the combination church and school. The men I had known so long were subdued and obviously troubled.

"My friends, I am confirming what you have already heard. Santa Anna has entered into Texas at the head of a large army supported by heavy artillery. General Urrea has crossed the Rio Grande at Matamoras leading a second army. General Houston has ordered the garrison at San Antonio to abandon the Alamo and withdraw east of the Colorado. He has ordered Colonel James Fannin at Goliad with four hundred men to abandon Fort Defiance and fall back. Houston believes we do not have the strength or the resources to defend fixed positions, but need to fight the Mexicans in the open where their advantage over us will not be so great. I personally agree with him."

"If General Cos with twelve hundred men and twenty cannon could not hold San Antonio against our four hundred men, what chance do the men at the Alamo have against an army of thousands with siege cannon? General Houston believes we should concentrate the Texan forces and fight on ground advantageous to us."

"I have received our orders from General Houston. We are to remain here at Navasota Crossing for two purposes.

"First, we are to deny the Mexican army the use of this crossing, should they penetrate this far. We are to maintain it for the use of the Texan army if needed".

"Second, we are to assist and protect settlers heading east away from the fighting. We cannot abandon them to the pursuit of the Mexican cavalry, and we cannot deny use of the Camino Real to the Texas army if it were to become impassable due to stranded settlers."

"The Upper Brazos Company is to do the same at Louisiana Landing. If they are overrun, they are to fall back here."

"Finally, we are ordered to be ready on instant notice to send the bulk of our regiment to support Houston's army when they finally make contact with the Mexican army, leaving only a rear guard to protect the crossing and assist settlers fleeing the fighting."

Chance stood and faced me. "We have always followed you, Colonel. What do we do now?"

"We wait. And we pray." And we did just that, there in the still quietness of our chapel. Texas and Texans would need many more prayers before the war was over.

A small band of volunteers from Tennessee arrived on the Camino Real late one afternoon. They camped in the meadow south of the settlement. They were led by Davy Crockett. He was a woodsman deluxe, bear hunting fool, congressman, fiddle player, Indian fighter, politician, world class tale teller, and the life of the party.

He and his men were headed to reinforce the Alamo. They had heard that it was the only garrison in Santa Anna's path to Texas, and they wanted to get there before the fighting was over. They would get their wish.

When they left the next morning, I rode along with them to Louisiana Landing on the Brazos. Crockett and I talked of many things during the long ride there. Actually, he did most of the talking and I did most of the listening. He was a philosopher, too. Most of his country bumpkin backwoodsman personality was a cover for the deeply thoughtful man that he really was. He knew the seriousness of their undertaking. He said he felt as if he were riding to fulfill his destiny.

The twin ferries moved them across the river to continue their fated journey. I was never to see them again.

18

February 1836, Washington-on-the-Brazos, Texas

AFTER CROCKET AND his men had left, Rob and I came down river on the steamer to Washington-on-the-Brazos, arriving February 27, 1836. Stephen Austin was still in the United States stirring up support in the form of cash, loans, arms, supplies and volunteers for Texas. General Houston was here at the third Convention, constantly bickering with the unlikable Provisional President, Henry Smith.

A frustrated Sam Houston ate supper with us that night on board the *Brazos Belle*. "Boys, I'm tellin' you that is the most fractious man I ever met. He would argue with a stump."

"What's got you so worked up, General?" Rob asked.

"Mostly the conduct of the war, Captain Rob. We can't defend fortified positions against the strength of the Mexican army. We'll only succeed by meeting the enemy on the field of battle where the conditions are favorable to us. I ordered the evacuation of the Alamo and Goliad, but Smith countermanded my orders. He is even diverting all our reinforcements to San Antonio."

"In January, I left James McNeill to demolish the Alamo. He reinforced it."

"Colonel Bowie and Colonel Travis arrived there with their volunteers and decided to defend it."

"Colonel Crockett and his men from Tennessee are there, too. When Neill's wife fell ill, he left Travis in charge. Travis and Bowie have had some kind of a quarrel, so now they have a joint command."

"General Houston, isn't there still time to move the men? Santa Anna isn't expected for a few more weeks."

"Colonel Turner, it sure gets formal with all of this General this, and Colonel that. I would be just plenty happy if you called me Sam except in command situations. May I just call the two of you Aaron and Rob?"

We nodded in agreement. It had made talking to him difficult.

"Aaron, Santa Anna and three thousand men are already across the Rio Grande! And General Urrea is marching on the Atascosito Road along the Texas coast."

We sat in stunned silence. Santa Anna himself was in Texas leading thousands of men.

"How many Texans are at the Alamo?"

"A few over a hundred and fifty under Jim Bowie. Travis is flat on his back with fever."

"Sam, Aaron and I were there with Burleson. There ain't no way one hundred and fifty men can hold him off. They're dead men."

"I know that, Rob. That's what has been under my skin so bad. Nobody will listen. Even if I march every man I've got and Fannin would leave Fort Defiance, we couldn't save them, and would lose it all at the same time. The best I can salvage from this is to evacuate everyone east and concentrate my forces. At least the Alamo can keep Santa Anna busy for a while. What a waste of men's lives! We'll pull Santa Anna far away from friendly country and away from his line of supply. We can beat him if we play it just right. God help Texas if I'm wrong."

The Convention was called to order March 1, 1836. The Alamo still held. Texas could not save the men there, and to do so would be suicide.

On March 2, a roll call vote was taken. We declared Texas a republic, free and independent of Mexico. A provisional government was formed pending elections, should we survive long enough to even hold elections. A constitution was written.

We existed as a nation on paper. We had an abundance of natural resources and tough settlers. We faced an angry dictator of a nation many times our size with immeasurably greater manpower and resources.

Santa Anna had raised a blood red flag from the San Fernando Church tower, the tallest structure in San Antonio. The flag indicated there would be no mercy, no quarter, no surrender, no prisoners, a fight to the death of the last combatant.

The vanguard of the Mexican army of eighteen hundred men assembled in San Antonio with only two six pounder cannon. But many more men and the mighty siege guns were pressing slowly northward to the fight.

The one hundred eighty-nine men of the Alamo could still cut and run. The Alamo was not surrounded. Messengers still rode in and out on a daily basis. But the men of the Alamo had come to fight. They had come to stay. In response to a last desperate call for help, thirty-two men from Gonzales had arrived under the command of Lieutenant Kimball.

James Fannin still tarried at Goliad with his four hundred and fifty men. It was possible that the arrival of a force of that size to the rear of the Mexican army could drive the Mexicans away, at least until their reinforcements arrived. It would have presented an opportunity for the defenders of the Alamo to counter attack, or at least escape. But Fannin knew General Urrea was marching on Goliad. He was reluctant to abandon Fort Defiance.

Word reached us that the Alamo had fallen. At a cost of six hundred Mexican lives, with the mournful sounds of the deguello playing on enemy trumpets, the embattled mission fell on March 6. The few surviving Texans were executed. A few non-combatant women, children and slaves were spared to spread the news.

As if things could not get worse, reports arrived that Fannin and all of his force had been captured and executed. Apparently, Fannin had belatedly decided to evacuate Goliad. He was encumbered with the heavy cannon he refused to leave behind.

On March 19, his force was caught in the open along Coleta Creek by Urrea's nineteen hundred men. After a sharp skirmish, Fannin surrendered. Under the direct orders of Santa Anna, and over the protests of General Urrea, the three hundred and fifty-two survivors had been lined up and executed on March 27. A handful had escaped during the chaos of the execution to tell the tale of terror. The effect on Texas was chilling. We were frightened. We were angry, very angry.

General Houston ordered the forces at Gonzales to fall back to the Brazos. This time, there was no argument. He called on all available militia to converge on his army as they retreated and regrouped to the east.

The Mexicans advanced in a three pronged attack. General Ramirez y Sesma led a cavalry brigade along the Camino Real in the northern-most wing of the attack. General Urrea proceeded along the coastal plain with the southern wing of the advance. Santa Anna personally led the central prong.

He pursued the fleeing provisional government and Sam Houston. If he could capture the legislative body or the executive branch, such as it was, the Texan rebellion might collapse. Failing that, he would annihilate the only Texas army of any size left in the field, the ever retreating General Houston. General Cos was to follow Santa Anna's column, but to be ready to reinforce either the north or south wing as necessary.

All Texan combatants were to be executed and their families exiled. Anglos who had not participated in the rebellion would be forcibly relocated to the interior of Mexico and their lands forfeit.

Foreign mercenaries, including Americans, would be hung as pirates. Abandoned Texan land would be redistributed to his victorious army. The Anglo-American stain on the Mexican province of Texas would be erased forever.

Settlers desperately tried to get away from the approaching armies, especially to reach the safety of the United States across the Sabine River. American troops had been moved to the Louisiana border to prevent any Mexican pursuit onto United States' sovereign territory. Thus began what forever would be known as "The Runaway Scrape."

By hand cart, horseback, wagon, and on foot, Texan families left with the clothes on their backs, a little food and almost nothing else. The roads were clogged with fleeing settlers desperate to get as far east as possible. Heavy rains and swollen rivers impeded their progress.

At each river crossing there were great delays as people had to wait their turn to cross on the over-burdened ferries. The ferries ran in shifts day and night without ceasing. Food supplies grew short, as did tempers.

Our militia at Navasota Crossing was able to keep order. We opened our stores of food to feed the hungry refugees. Each day more cattle were slaughtered for food, and barrels of corn meal were baked into bread by our valiant women. They were not ready to leave yet.

We restarted the grist mill to grind more meal each day from the dried corn we had saved for our livestock. It was urgently needed by these desperate Texans. If we survived, it was close enough to spring green up that the livestock would be fine.

Diseases of all nature hit these poor folks like a hammer. They were not able to stop to treat the stricken. Many of their dead were hurriedly buried in our cemetery. One of the refugees told me things were much the same at Louisiana Landing where the twin ferries and the *Brazos Belle* moved more people than we were able to do. However, the Navasota was still able to be forded by those who were mounted, so this helped the congestion considerably.

Our orders were immediate and clear. Rob's Upper Brazos militia was to hold the Brazos crossing there at all cost, including burning the ferries if necessary, and to assist the refugees as long as possible. If they were overrun, they were to fall back on the Navasota Crossing and pursue the same policy there.

My force was to hold the river crossing, deny its use to the Mexican army should they reach that far, then to fall back to the Trinity. In the meantime, we were to help eliminate the bottleneck of refugees there. In a day, we had built a second ferry and had it operational, drawn by our good mules. It helped the congestion tremendously.

Cody Teel was in command of a scouting party to screen for Mexican troops between the Brazos River and the Navasota to give us an early warning of their approach. It was a dangerous job, but Cody took it with his usual good humor, even though Miranda was brought to tears.

We built log barricades on the east bank of the Navasota at the crossing to protect us if the Mexican cavalry should penetrate this far. We kept our rifles covered with oiled leather to keep the flintlocks dry; they were never far from our sides.

Nancy brought me coffee and hot food as I tried to make order out of the near chaos across the river. "Aaron, I have our bags packed and the best wagon loaded. In the morning we're hitching our six best mules to the wagon and heading east. Marcus and Lucius are going with us on horseback. Your place is here. We'll wait for you at the Campos farm near Nacogdoches as long as we can."

My eyes filled with tears. I had not even thought about them leaving. They should have already left.

"I thought I was bringing you to the 'promised land.' Look what it has become." I grabbed her and hugged her tightly.

"Aaron, you need to talk to the other settlers here. They look up to you."

Calling our friends and neighbors to me, I stood in the bed of a wagon and spoke as loudly as I could. "Friends, God has not led us to this place to die. He has a plan for us, not to do us harm, but good. We need to trust Him in all that we do. In the morning Nancy and my children and grandchildren will be leaving for safety in the east. Marcus and Lucius will ride with any who choose to go for protection. Any of the married men who feel they need to go are excused from militia duty, no questions asked. I will stay here to see what I can do to stop Santa Anna. Follow your own consciences. Leave if you must, stay if you can. God bless us all. God bless Sam Houston, and God bless Texas!"

19

April 1836, Groce's Plantation, lower Brazos River, Texas

HOUSTON'S ARMY TOOK a more southerly line of retreat. When they had reached San Felipe from Gonzales, the steamer *Yellowstone* was able to move the entire army over the Brazos in a few hours. They followed the east bank of the Brazos to Jared Groce's plantation where they would have time to recoup and eat a few hot meals.

Santa Anna himself was leading the central column, directly in pursuit of Houston's retreating army. He recalled all of Sesma's troops to consolidate with his army, leaving only a screen of cavalry on the Camino Real. General Urrea continued to push almost unopposed along the coast. A small detail of Texans had been assigned to fell trees across the roads and delay Urrea's progress without engaging his troops.

Santa Anna's column was slowed by heavy rains which swelled creeks and rivers. The dirt roads turned into bottomless mud tracks. He was eventually forced to abandon most of his heavy artillery and much of his supply train.

Houston had finally gone to ground at Groce's plantation. Reinforcements slipped in from the west, evading the Mexican forces. Militia units both large and small flocked to Houston's camp from all of Texas east of the Brazos. Volunteers from the United States marched down the Camino Real, bucking the tide of fleeing settlers. More arrived by ship along the coast at Anahuac and Galveston.

Two beautiful six pounder cannon arrived from the citizens of Cincinnati, Ohio. They had been sent down the Ohio River to the Mississippi, from New Orleans to Brazosport, then up the Brazos by steamboat to Houston's camp. They were affectionately called "The Twin Sisters." They were the only artillery Sam Houston possessed.

General Houston had assembled about twelve hundred men when our orders arrived at Navasota Crossing. Because of the diminished threat along the Camino Real, I was to leave only enough men to work the ferries and guard them against Mexican patrols. The remainder of my regiment was to report immediately to Houston's camp.

We left twenty men behind to tend the ferries and the still flowing stream of refugees. I placed them under the command of Joe Morgan. His son, Logan would hear nothing of staying behind, nor would Tanner or Gray. Logan's scar glowed red on his cheek, showing he was a battle scarred veteran.

One hundred of us rode to Louisiana Landing in one day, and left our horses under the care of William Applewhite. As before, he would command the twenty men remaining there. Rob joined us with the other forty men of his company. We did not wait to eat or drink, but immediately boarded the *Brazos Belle*. It was standing room only, but we didn't care. This was the fastest way to reach General Houston. We were at Groce's plantation by daylight.

Once we were there, Cody Teel discovered his adopted son, Will Smith Teel, had slipped himself unnoticed into our group. The boy was a skinny teenager who had lost his family to the Comanche.

He had been saved by Cody's bravery and good shooting. "I come to kill Meskins, Reverend. I ain't gonna go back even if you whup me."

"Will, that ain't no way to talk to your elders! Colonel, I don't know what to do with him. He got himself a pair of saddle pistols, a tomahawk, and a good rifle. You know I was fighting Indians before I was as old as him. I haven't got a way to get him home."

"Cody, you were only a thirteen year old kid when you rode to Texas with me in 1817. You handled yourself well. You were fifteen when you killed the Comanche that was stealing Will."

"Will, you look at me, son. I'm not happy you are here, but there are others not much older than you. You stick close to Cody and don't give me any trouble or any more sass."

"So I can stay to fight?"

"I guess you can, boy."

"Yes sir, then I'm gonna show you how to do it!"

Cody and I looked at each other. Cody smiled a nervous smile. "I'll try to take care of him."

We moved south and east. Each night in camp around the cooking fires, there was speculation as to Houston's plan. Some wondered if he even had one. One theory was that he was trying to retreat all the way to the Sabine and the safety of American troops just across the river. A Mexican attack there would force the United States into a war. A few pessimists thought Houston was just running anywhere he could go to get away from Santa Anna. And some of us thought General Houston was drawing Santa Anna ever deeper into hostile territory, farther and farther from his supplies, looking for the ideal place and time to turn and fight.

The almost daily rains and soggy conditions added to our misery. At least we were well supplied. A boat carrying Mexican martial goods, food and ammunition had been captured on the Brazos. We were feasting while the Mexicans scavenged for food in an unfriendly territory.

Our scouts indicated that Santa Anna seemed to be intent on

capturing the fleeing government of Texas before they could reach the relative safety of Galveston Island. That being the case, Harrisburg looked pretty close to where we would intersect the Mexican army.

Measles and dysentery affected some of our ranks. They were sent back to recuperate at Jared Groce's plantation. The rest of us kept marching through the mud.

"Deaf" Smith reported the Mexicans had burned Harrisburg and were moving along the west bank of the San Jacinto River. The government had escaped to Galveston by the skin of their teeth. On the morning of April 19, General Sam Houston addressed us.

"Men, you have been patient. You will soon see battle. Remember the Alamo! Remember Goliad!"

Those few, powerful words so stirred our blood that the discomforts of the march were forgotten. We did remember the Alamo! We did remember what the Mexicans had done at Goliad. We would never forget. There was a score to be settled that required payment in Mexican blood. It was our intention to see that it was paid in full.

He positioned us along a timbered ridge near the juncture of Buffalo Bayou with the San Jacinto River. Our excess baggage and supplies were left behind near the smoldering remains of Harrisburg, guarded by those who had recently fallen ill. There were two hundred and forty-eight too sick to fight. They could still fire a rifle well enough to form our rear guard.

There were nine hundred and ten men and boys fit for duty. Nine hundred and ten angry, determined men awaited the "Napoleon of the West."

Santa Anna's army of seven hundred men had arrived and set up camp three quarters of a mile inland from an oxbow bend of the San Jacinto River. Marshland and a brackish body of deep water called Peggy's Lake were immediately behind the weary army, and beyond that, the banks of the deep, impassable San Jacinto.

His tired and ill-fed men dragged up fallen branches and pack saddles to form a makeshift breast works. Their fatigue, and contempt for their Texan enemies, convinced them there was no need to send out soldiers for picket line duty, and only a few exhausted sentries were set to keep watch.

Colonel Sherman led a probing body of cavalry to fully determine the Mexican position. His troop was challenged by a small body of Mexican infantry in a brief pitched skirmish. Sherman withdrew his cavalry to avoid springing the trap before it was set.

I addressed the members of my regiment that I knew so well, as they sat frying bacon and corn cakes for supper in small groups. "Clean and oil your guns. We'll need them tomorrow."

Many of the men gladly accepted my offer to pray with them.

I found Logan, Tanner, and Gray. Their enthusiasm for battle had been tempered at the siege of San Antonio. Their youthful eagerness had been replaced by the grim, brutal reality of the job at hand. "I want all three of you knot heads to make me proud of you all over again tomorrow, but I want every one of you marching back home with me when this is over."

I finally came to the fire shared by Nick, Cody, Chance and Rob, my companions for the past nineteen years. The three youths who had joined Rob and me on the Camino Real in 1817 had grown into hardened men of the frontier. Rob and I had both been aged by the trials of our life in Texas. I was now fifty-three. We had encountered everything Texas had thrown at us and survived. Whatever presented tomorrow, we were ready to meet the challenge head on.

The next morning, "Deaf" Smith galloped into camp while we were finishing our breakfast in the pre-dawn fog. General Cos and the rear guard of five hundred men had crossed the only bridge over Buffalo Bayou and would soon join Santa Anna.

A murmur arose from many of the men that we should immediately attack before their forces could join. Those with some military experience pointed out the danger of engaging an enemy while another was uncontained on your flank. Houston smiled. He actually smiled at the news!

"We will let them join forces, and smite them together. Burn the bridge on Buffalo Bayou! Render Lynch's Ferry unavailable to our enemy!" There would be no easy line of retreat for either the Mexican army or for us. "We will conquer or we will perish! We must act now or abandon all hope."

April 21, 1836, dawned clear and sunny. The mists of this low land were burned away by the morning sun. The army under our old enemy, General Cos, arrived and settled in about noon. Cooking fires were lit as the hungry Mexican soldiers cooked what corn they had left into tortillas. The breeze carried the scent of the wood and the hot food to our position.

Houston already had us in our line of battle formation. The center was under the command of Colonel Edward Burleson. We were attached to his command. To our left was infantry under Colonel Sherman. Immediately to our right stood the "Twin Sisters" and the men detailed to fire them. Further right was a body of infantry commanded by Colonel Millard. Out on the far right flank, was what cavalry we possessed. They were commanded by Mirabeau B. Lamar, a volunteer from Georgia. The previous day, he had been a simple private. But because of his bravery in the previous day's skirmish, he had been given a field promotion to commander of the cavalry detachment.

All of us were dressed in homespun or buckskins. The only uniformed troop on the field was a company of volunteers known as the "Kentucky Rifles." Juan Sequin's mounted vaqueros were attached to Lamar's cavalry. They wore white arm bands and placed playing cards around the bands of their hats to distinguish them in battle from the enemy.

Rob and his company were near me in line, as was a company under Chance. On the other side was a company under Nick's command, assisted by his brother, Cody. Close to Cody's side was young Will. I had Logan, Tanner and Gray directly at my side.

By mid-afternoon, we strode out of the protection of the timbered ridge and began our advance toward the Mexican lines. We moved steadily forward, sweeping across the prairie with the men bending low to utilize the cover of the rolling terrain. The "Twin Sisters" were pulled by man ropes until they were within close range of the enemy position. A single fife struck up marching music. The Mexicans still had not thrown out a skirmish line or stationed sentries. We advanced unnoticed to within deathly close range. The line halted. The cannon were muscled into position.

On Houston's order, the cannon belched forth their deadly charge of hundreds of musket balls, chains and horse shoes. The whole Texan line surged forward screaming "Remember the Alamo! Remember Goliad!" We opened a withering fire. Mexicans, who had stood when they heard our shouts, were cut down like ripe wheat before a scythe. We did not stop to reload, but charged the breastworks with our rifles as clubs.

The astonished Mexicans began to fall back on their own men and were unable to mount an organized defense. Nick and Cody seized a single Mexican cannon and wheeled it around to fire point blank into the fleeing enemy.

A group of Mexican soldiers tried to form up in front of me, but we took them down with our saddle pistols before they could fire. Returning our empty pistols to our belts, we resumed our pursuit with our rifles as brutally effective clubs.

The Mexicans broke and ran for the rear, trampling their comrades. They stopped at the edge of the swampy marshland. Some turned to fire, but most plunged into the mud. Logan took down a Mexican corporal with a mighty swing of his rifle. Tanner reloaded his pistols, and dropped two soldiers who had turned to fight. Gray slashed with his tomahawk and knife like a mad man, wounding or killing all who stood before him.

All were swept before us. We pushed into the marsh to continue pursuit, reloading as we charged. Many of the Mexicans had discarded their weapons as they ran. Many muskets had been left stacked in their camp, never retrieved by their owners.

I saw young Will pursuing a group of fleeing soldiers. He shot one with his rifle and two with his pistols. He ran at another with his rifle raised as a club, only to be impaled by an enemy bayonet in his chest. As the soldier put his foot on the dying boy's chest to retrieve his bayonet, Cody shot the Mexican dead with a rifle ball to the face. It was too late for Will. His anger, festering for so many years, was finally spent with his last breath.

As we watched at the edge of Peggy's Lake, the remaining Mexicans plunged into the murky water to escape. Many of the struggling men drowned. Those who did not presented easy targets for the riflemen along the bank. The fury of the Texans could not be contained. The hounds of war had not yet been satisfied.

Some of the Mexican cavalry tried to escape to the Buffalo Bayou bridge, only to find it destroyed. Plunging their horses into the deep swift water, many of the horses and their desperate riders drowned. Those who did not drown were shot by our pursuing cavalrymen. There was no escape.

Their anger and blind fury finally spent, the Texans gradually gave up their assault. They began rounding up the surviving enemy soldiers. The 'butcher's bill" was enormous. There had been six hundred and thirty Mexican soldiers killed, two hundred and eight wounded, and seven hundred and thirty taken prisoner. We had suffered nine Texans killed, including Will, and thirty wounded. Besides the prisoners, we captured huge numbers of muskets, pistols, horses, mules, supplies and twelve thousand silver pesos. The day was ours.

20

April 1836, San Jacinto River, Texas

SAM HOUSTON HAD been shot in the ankle. He rested in the shade of a great live oak tree as his field commanders confirmed the overwhelming results. Santa Anna was not to be found.

Late in the afternoon, a Texan captured a tattered Mexican in a private's uniform, crawling on his hands and knees through the tall grass. He herded him onto the battlefield with the other prisoners. To the astonishment of the Texans, many of the Mexican prisoners began to salute the ragged private and address him as "El Presidente."

He was immediately brought to Houston where he lay recovering from his wound. With an attempt at arrogance, the prisoner introduced himself. "I am General Antonio Lopez de Santa Anna, President of the Republic of Mexico. I am a prisoner of war, at your disposition." Houston gave him a cold response. He sent for me as interpreter. I introduced myself to the fallen aggressor.

"General, I am Lieutenant Colonel Aaron Turner. We have met before when you commanded at Vera Cruz."

"I do not know you. What has an emperor to do with a peasant like you?"

Feeling the blood rise in my cheeks, I dug in my pocket for an oiled leather pouch. From the pouch I pulled a smaller, stained silk bag. From the bag, I produced a gold medallion. He had given it to me at Vera Cruz many years ago. I rolled it in my fingers and handed it to him. "Perhaps this will refresh your memory."

He studied the medallion which bore his likeness. He looked at me again, studying my face. "Yes, I remember you well. I find that I am once again in your debt and at your mercy."

"Mercy?" Houston shouted in anger. "Mercy? What claim do you have to mercy? Where was your mercy at the Alamo? Where was your mercy at Goliad? I should turn you over to their widows and orphans and allow them to beat you to death."

Rob, Chance, Cody, Nick and I crowded around the defeated general to protect him from those who shouted for his death. I allowed General Houston to regain his composure before I spoke. "General Houston, a live president is worth far more to Texas than a dead general."

Houston reacted quickly. "Colonel Turner is right. You other men stand down. As much as it galls me, he will live."

After two hours of talking and interpreting, Santa Anna agreed to order all Mexican troops in Texas to immediately withdraw south of the Rio Grande. As President of the Republic of Mexico, he would recognize the independence of the Republic of Texas. Couriers were sent out with multiple copies of his orders to any and all Mexican troops remaining in Texas. Our Navasota regiment was assigned as a special guard to Santa Anna.

With heavy hearts we laid Will to rest there on the battlefield before we left. Cody was deeply shaken by the loss. Rob's company was to march back to Groce's plantation and retrieve the *Brazos Belle*, then meet us at Velasco.

General Urrea sharply protested the orders from his commanding officer and president, but he marched his troops back to Matamoras. The other smaller bodies of troops were shocked by the news, but quickly obeyed. Following the departure of the remnants of the Mexican army from Texas, the volunteer Texan army began to disband and return home.

Once at Velasco, Santa Anna signed a treaty recognizing the independence of Texas from Mexico and agreed to pay damages to Texas for the war. Multiple copies of the Treaty of Velasco were signed and sent to Mexico, Texas and the United States.

Our services were no longer needed. We began to board the *Brazos Belle* for our trip back up the Brazos and our journey home. Santa Anna thanked me for my intervention which had spared his life. At this point I could not express the contempt I felt for the man. I coldly shook his extended hand and left without a word.

As I walked up the gangway onto the stern-wheeler, I paused to think. I had been the last one to climb aboard. I walked toward the great churning paddles. I reached deep within my pocket and pulled out the pouch I had carried for so many years. I rolled the heavy gold medallion in my hand and studied it closely. I walked to the back of the steamer and threw the medallion into the churning river.

I had lost my precious double-barreled Manton rifle at the Battle of San Jacinto. I had broken the stock over the head of a Mexican soldier and had hurled the pieces into Peggy's Lake. It had belonged to my grandfather and had been one of my most valued possessions. However, I knew Grandfather Thomas Turner would have approved of the way it had been used.

Our regiment was quiet, but in good spirits as we reached Louisiana Landing. There was a victory celebration that night, but my heart ached to be home.

Early the next morning, after retrieving the horses we had left behind, we saddled up and rode hard for the Navasota. We arrived just before dark. Having been forewarned of our return, they had prepared a feast for us.

We were home, safer than when we had left it, weary of war and sick of bloodshed. Nancy and the children, along with Marcus, Lucius and their families, had been home for over two weeks. They had gone as far as Nacogdoches and stayed with our friends, the Campos.

Logan, Gray and Tanner had been boys when we had ridden away to the siege of San Antonio. Now, they had survived San Jacinto, boys no longer. They had lost something good and innocent in those few months. It its place was a toughness that would guide them all their lives.

I held each of my children and grandchildren in turn. I was doing well until I hugged Nancy. All the emotions of the past years and months rose up like a fountain. I held her and sobbed.

We had come to Texas years before and built a home where there had been nothing. We had endured disease and depredation by Indians. We had struggled and survived. We had rejoiced to see ourselves become full citizens of Mexico, only to see Mexico descend into civil war and dictatorship. We had seen the fury of the "Napoleon of the West" turned against us, and emerged as citizens of a new, independent republic.

Had peace finally come to our prosperous promised land? Or would the hounds of war return again to our door? Would Texas ever truly be tamed and know peace?

That night as I sat with Nancy once again on the gallery, I saw a single brilliant falling star. The quarter moon seemed to smile in knowing silence. The gentle southwestern breeze whispered through the newly leafed trees. The bobwhites called from the meadow. I could hear their voices, but I could not understand their message. But I did know Texas. Texas would not go gently into that good night. I knew in my heart that the price for peace had not yet been paid in full.

Glossary

Alcalde: roughly the equivalent of an American mayor, but with broader authority; the alcalde could be appointed by the ayuntamiento, or town council, or by higher authorities; the alcalde served as the head of the civilian government of a city or larger political unit; the alcalde served as a judge in both civil and criminal cases

Ayuntamiento: (i un tam e in' toh) under Mexican law, a town council; it could be elected, but was often appointed

Centralist: a political philosophy favoring strong central government over the rights of states, cities and individuals; the opposite of a federalist philosophy

Comanche Moon: the month beginning with the first full moon in October; this was the time most favored by Comanche for raiding

Deguello: (day gway' yoh) a military melody played on trumpets indicating the impending doom of an enemy, especially when no quarter was to be given

Duwali: also known as Chief Bowls, High Chief of the Cherokee in Texas and personal friend of Sam Houston

Escopeta: (es co pe' tah) a large caliber smoothbore musket used by the Spanish and Mexican armies; they ranged from .54 to .79 caliber, with .69 being the most common; they were notoriously inaccurate beyond seventy yards; they were durable and heavy, and ideal for use in close combat with a bayonet

Federalist: a political philosophy favoring decentralized government, with relatively strong state governments and a proportionally weaker central government; the rights of the individual were more important than the government

Filibusters: mercenary adventurers, hired ruffians

Fredonian Republic: a short-lived illegal movement started by the Edwards brothers in Nacogdoches which attempted to claim political independence from Mexico and to illegally seize all the land in Texas from the Sabine to the Colorado River; the Fredonian revolt was put down by prompt action by the militia from Austin's Colony acting on behalf of the Mexican government

Fresno: a type of road work implement powered by draft animals used to level roads, and also to dig trenches, ditches and ponds

Gelding: a neutered male equine, especially applied to a horse; geldings tend to be calmer and easier to handle than stallions

Gilt: a young female hog

Grippe: an obsolete term for any flu-like illness

Hacienda: an elegant Spanish or Mexican residence, particularly a rural residence; term also applies to the land surrounding and supporting the hacienda

Hidalgo: a Spanish term for a gentleman, particularly of the landed gentry

John mule: a male mule, usually referring to a neutered male mule

Labor: a Spanish measurement of land equal to one hundred and seventy seven acres

League: a Spanish unit of land measurement equal to four thousand four hundred and twenty-eight acres; also a distance of roughly 2.6 miles

Molly mule: a female mule

Mordida: Spanish for "a little bite", meaning a bribe or tip for faster or better service; these were considered perfectly proper

Morral: a crudely made bag with carrying straps usually made from grass, fiber or coarse cloth

Nacogdoches: (nac ah doh' chez): an important settlement in eastern Texas on the Camino Real

Natchitoches: (nac' ah tosh): an important center of trade at the junction of the Camino Real and the Red River in Louisiana

Pannier: a canvas or leather cargo container made to fit pack saddles

Postern gate: a small gate from a fortified position to allow limited access for ordinary mundane chores without endangering the main gate; the postern gate, if not well guarded presented a vulnerable place in a fort's walls

Soldado: a Spanish term for a common soldier

Suggested Reading

Campbell, Randolph B. *Gone to Texas: a history of the Lone Star State.* New York: Oxford University Press. 2003

Cantrell, Gregg. *Stephen F. Austin, Empresario of Texas.* New Haven: Yale University Press. 1999

Crisp, James E. *Sleuthing the Alamo.* New York: Oxford University Press. 2005

Fehrenbach, T.R. *Lone Star: A History of Texas and Texans.* New York: Collier Books. 1968

Hardin, Stephen L. *Texian Iliad.* Austin, Texas: University of Texas Press. 1994

LaVere, David. *The Texas Indians.* College Station, Texas: Texas A&M University Press. 2004

Meyers, Michael C.; Sherman, William L.; Deeds, Susan M. *The Course of Mexican History, Seventh Edition.* New York: Oxford University Press. 1985

Miller, Robert R. *Mexico, A History.* Norman, Oklahoma: University of Oklahoma Press. 1985

Newcomb, W. W., Junior. *The Indians of Texas.* Austin, Texas: University of Texas Press. 1985

Teja, Jesus F. de la. *San Antonio de Bexar.* Albuquerque, New Mexico: University of New Mexico Press. 1995

Genealogy

Thomas Turner, born Ireland, circa 1732; died South Carolina, 1794 or 1796 (records conflict) = Priscella Alexander

Thomas Turner, Jr. born Marlboro County, South Carolina, 1751; died Marlboro County, South Carolina, 1822 = Rebekah (also recorded as Rebecca), last name not recorded

Aaron Turner, born Marlboro County, South Carolina, 1783; Died Leon County, Texas, December 18, 1851 = Nancy King, date undetermined, Georgia

Aaron Lloyd Turner, born Leon County, Texas, December 17, 1850; died February 22, 1939, Brownfield, Terry County, Texas = Ella Fisher

John Karr Turner, born Moro, Taylor County, Texas, December 12, 1890; died Seagraves, Gaines County, Texas, June 1, 1964 = Effie Beatrice Turner

Aaron Lynn Turner, born Seagraves, Gaines County, Texas, May 2, 1931 = Doris Alene Combs

Stephen Lynn Turner, born Fayetteville, Washington County, Arkansas, January 10, 1957 = Roberta Ann Lyles

Melissa Ruth Turner, born September 12, 1984, Lubbock, Lubbock county, Texas = Dustin Alan DeBusk

Aaron Lyles Turner, born January 19, 1988, Plainview, Hale County, Texas = Sarah M. Robinson